a passionate development

ELEANOR HILL

Published in 2003 by Onlywomen Press, Limited, London, UK.

With financial support from Arts Council England

ISBN 0-906500-68-0

British Library Cataloguing-in-Publication Data.
A Catalogue record for this book is available from the British Library.

Typeset by Chris Fayers, Cardigan, Wales.
Printed and bound in Great Britain by Mackays of Chatham Limited.

For
Celia, Tony, Kwame and Ama
who keep Ghana so vividly alive
and
for my grandmother
who sparked my own passion for development

Part One: *Rainfall on Parched Ground*.

<u>1</u>

Fiona bent to lift the metal bucket and then strained against its weight as she staggered up the steep path. With a final heave, she emptied the water into the waiting barrel. Leaning against the back of the truck, she wiped her hand across her forehead leaving a streak of dirt. Sweat trickled steadily down between her shoulders. She watched the other women. Even after two years she was still amazed by their strength and poise. They swung the buckets up onto their heads as if they were only empty plastic and walked smoothly up the treacherous path to empty the water from them in one flowing movement. Watching them was hypnotic.

"I'm getting worse," Fiona spoke as the last bucketful sloshed into the barrel. "I managed to do six trips when we came down on Thursday, and today I'm done in after four. I don't know how you keep going."

Felicia, Comfort B and Kittewaa smiled at her, flexing their aching shoulders. "We're used to it, Sister Fiona." Comfort B replied. "That's the only difference."

Fiona looked at Kittewaa whose name reflected her physique, "But you're half my size and you can still beat me. It's shameful, that's what it is, shameful." She shrugged and climbed in behind the wheel of the truck. The others piled in beside her. "At least this is something I can do better," she said laughing, as she put the vehicle into first gear.

This trip down the escarpment had become a regular event over the last couple of months as the dry season extended, and the promised rain did not materialise. The harmattan wind blowing down from the Sahara in the north seemed to be emptying the whole desert on top of them, the dust was so thick. Every two or three days she drove some of the staff down to fill

5

up the three barrels which were the main water supply for the compound, providing water for the maternity ward, the outpatient building, which was now a temporary malnutrition ward, and for her house. Even after it had been boiled and filtered twice the water kept its earthy flavour. After the effort it took to collect, Fiona was keen to spill as little as possible of the water on the pot-holed road back to the compound.

The air was full of ash again. Another fire. Whenever there was a rumour that rain was on the way, some of the villagers would set off to prepare their farms for planting by burning off the undergrowth, the simplest and cheapest means of enriching the over-used soil. In the dry conditions, the fires easily spread out of control so that both day and night were punctuated by the booming thunder- cracks of falling trees. Fiona sometimes felt it was like living in a war zone. Arguing against this burning was one of Kofi Paul's priorities just now.

Thinking of Kofi Paul made her smile. She'd been talking to him about the impending evaluation visit by staff from ActionFirst's headquarters near Birmingham. ActionFirst Development provided almost all the funding for the project.

"I don't think we have any worries about the project," Fiona had said. "We score pretty highly on most of their buzz-words. But the visit will be important in shaping the future. We have to focus on sustainability."

Kofi Paul had chuckled. "So long as they can sustain me, I don't mind about the rest. Fufu three times a day, that's all I ask." Like many Ghanaians, Kofi Paul felt he had not eaten unless the meal included fufu, a mix of parboiled yam or cassava and plantain, pounded into a dough that Fiona privately thought of as a sort of pale green cement. He became serious. "We need to make them look at their part in the sustainability of what we do. What sort of partnership is it going to be? And I know Leo will focus on the value for money aspect. When I went on that course last year, it was clear his priority is economic viability."

"But it's achieving that without letting go of everything else. ActionFirst is still interested in other priorities too."

"Remind me again, how long are they here for?" he'd asked.

"They're in the country for about a month, but they'll only be here in Osubuso for four days, according to this." Fiona had held out the letter which announced the visit. "They've got to visit four other projects, including one up in Bolga. We're next to last on the itinerary. They go up there after us."

"That's good," Kofi Paul had nodded, reading quickly through the information. "That means they'll already have something to compare us with, an idea of what's possible, but they won't be focused entirely on getting home. We should come out favourably against the Asomto project, at least." He paused. "Four days, what d'you think we should get them to focus on while they're here?"

Fiona replied, "What do you think? You know I can't plan this without your help." Kofi Paul's key role in the project had been confirmed within days of Fiona's arrival.

The two of them thrashed out a skeleton programme, which was added to and refined by the other senior staff. Osubuso was an integrated development project with a number of strands of which the best developed were the clinical and agricultural activities. The other activities included out-of-school and youth clubs, a few young men's groups and several women's co-operatives. Fiona encouraged all the staff to integrate their different activities, doubling up on resources whenever they could.

As well as being overall project manager, she took on some of the clinical work. Agnes and Comfort Atta were both qualified midwives but the remaining clinical staff were not professionally qualified, although increasingly able. To make the workload manageable, Fiona rotated on-call duties. The clinic did not have a general inpatient ward, only a maternity unit that had twelve beds and a labour room. But it was a busy unit, keeping the three of them fully occupied.

The remaining senior staff member was also called Kofi. He was a teacher by profession and in charge of the educational activities. Occasionally, to distinguish him from Kofi Paul, they used his nickname, Kofi-tumtum, but usually he was simply Kofi. As with Kittewaa, the nickname reflected a physical characteristic: 'tumtum' was Twi for black. Kofi was the blackest man she, and it appeared the majority of the staff, knew. Twi was not an easy language to the untrained ear. It had taken Fiona some months to understand that the meaning of the sounds she

7

heard was dependent on the intonation given to each syllable. She still struggled with anything other than basic conversation.

A series of potholes brought Fiona's attention back to her driving. It was already dusk by the time the truck lurched unevenly over the entrance to the compound and Fiona drew it to a halt opposite the maternity ward. It would remain there until the barrels were empty. She thanked the other women and went inside the house carrying one final bucket for herself. She needed a wash.

She had become expert at bathing in just one bowl of water. Theoretically her house had piped water but even without the drought the supply was erratic, and it was a long time since she'd bothered to try the tap. The electricity suffered from similar problems: black outs were common and on most days the current was reduced in power. *'What wouldn't I give for a piping hot power-shower?* she thought ruefully. To wash her hair in running water again would be ecstasy; at the moment she never quite felt she got all the dust out. She used a flannel to wet her body squeezing the drops back into the bowl, then soaped thoroughly, washing this off with the flannel again before tipping the contents of the bowl over her body for a final rinse.

She was due a long weekend off. Maybe she'd go down to stay in Accra once the visit was over. It was a while since she'd seen Rebecca and David. Their company, and that of their two lively children was a good tonic. Even better they never minded when she turned up unannounced. There was a telephone booth in town but often, by the time Fiona remembered, it would be past eleven at night and too late to call.

<u>2</u>

Imogen tried to hold herself steady as the Landrover Discovery lurched over a series of bumps, but it was difficult. This trip had taught her that being a passenger did not mean being passive; it took a lot of energy to ride these bumpy roads. After a while she'd stopped apologising to Keith and Leo each time she rocked into them. At least they were softer than the door or window frames, from which she had collected a few bruises when sudden jolts caught her unawares. It might have been easier if they were all bigger, she reflected, then they would have been wedged tight. Nigel, being the boss, rode in the front, and to be fair he would have struggled to fold his six and a half feet into the rear seats, Imogen thought.

The trip was not proving to be as enjoyable as she'd hoped. There was a level of tension between Nigel and Leo which gave an edge to most exchanges. She felt under constant scrutiny as she tried to avoid seeming to takes sides. Although his ideas on development were stimulating, Nigel irritated her with his patronising, avuncular manner. Leo engaged with her more as an equal in any debate, but appeared completely in thrall to hardline economic theory. She'd suggested to him that if developing countries reneged on their enormous debts, the only thing to happen would be a little discomfort for the wealthy. He'd nearly blown a gasket. Keith, the fourth member of the team, was much gentler but seemed unwilling to take part in anything like the lively, free-ranging discussions Imogen longed for.

ActionFirst Development had existed for just under ten years. It supported projects in southeast Asia and west Africa, with hopes for expansion into other sub-Saharan countries. It was not a big development organisation but it was gaining an excellent reputation for innovative and effective work. Health, agriculture, education and small scale economic development were the threads which ran through every project proposal. In the same way, self-sufficiency, equity and participation were key words in the vocabulary used by ActionFirst's staff. Imogen felt she could work within the organisation without compromising any of her own strongly held beliefs. She'd jumped at the chance of a second assignment with them.

Her mind went back to her first assignment in Bangladesh six months previously. Despite her long standing interest in development causes, it was the first time she'd been in close proximity to real poverty. The two of them had arrived in Dhaka just as the serious nature of the monsoon flooding became apparent. Already bewildered by the sheer number of people, the beggars, the traffic fumes and bustling chaos of the city, the reality of living with the floods hit Imogen like a hammer blow. One of the projects they visited was situated in a badly affected slum area. To reach it meant sitting in a small boat for almost an hour, instead of the ten minute drive it would normally have been. As the boatman poled them through the stinking water Imogen had looked around. What had been streets were waist deep, or more, in black greasy water.

"It's been this way for over a month, now." Rubia, the project worker who escorted them had spoken quietly. "If it gets any deeper, then the power and water supplies may be cut off altogether. Even now it's hard to cook, or get clean water."

The stench filled her nostrils as Imogen remembered. But, as vivid as the awfulness she'd witnessed, was the memory of how the people were simply getting on with their normal daily life. The shops remained open, with owners sitting cross-legged on top of their counters and customers standing in the waist deep water while they made their purchases, or bargaining from a boat drawn up in the doorway. The more forward thinking, or those with the resources for it, had built temporary brick walls across their doors to try and keep out the water, but many just moved their stock onto higher shelves. Hawkers plied their wares, calling loudly as they waded through the inky flood-water. And the children were definitely enjoying it. They leapt and dived, shrieked and yelled, their eyes shining and teeth gleaming. Where vehicles could still get through the flooded roads, the children body-surfed on their bow waves, or caught hold of passing bumpers to hitch a free ride. Imogen found it unbearable to think of the additional danger such gleeful delight brought with it.

As a photographer, Imogen was in her element. Almost every-where she turned there was an irresistible image. But as a human being she was cut to the quick. She had vowed there and then, in the boat, that she would go much further in her efforts to help bring about a world in which this level of suffering could not occur.

Martine, her lover of the moment, had arranged for her to be the official photographer on that trip. Martine worked at ActionFirst on their southeast Asia desk as the regional gender officer. She made regular visits to Bangladesh, India and Thailand to check up on the projects ActionFirst funded. Imogen loved to listen when she got into full flow about the inequities of the patriarchal world and what must be done to address the situation. Her eyes would flash and she punctuated her speeches with dramatic gestures. "There is no excuse" was her motto. Martine never let a statement pass unchallenged. To her, development was synonymous with the struggle for political power and its attainment would only come through the equitable distribution of that power. It was a shame Martine wasn't on this second trip, Imogen thought sadly. She missed that energy and enthusiasm, and none of her current companions appeared to have an atom of it.

But here she was, and the contrast could not be greater. "*From flood to drought in one easy movement*". Instead of oceans of polluted water, here the problem was none at all. It was a world of dust. A fine powder overlay everything, almost obscuring the sun in an ochre haze. It filled her eyes, ears and mouth making her feel permanently filthy. The taste of it in her mouth was almost familiar now after two weeks in the country, but she still couldn't stand the sensation of grit between her teeth.

Glancing out of the car, she was startled to see white flakes floating past the window. The vehicle was climbing upwards through bush interspersed with patches of farmland. Every few yards, it seemed, they passed a swathe of smouldering ground, some debris still flaring into flame. The black, burnt stumps of trees were stark outlines against the soft drifts of grey ash. It was the ash swirling in the wind which had caught her eye. This wasn't the luxuriant, green African forest she'd been led to expect. Imogen's thoughts raced back and forth between Bangladesh and Ghana.

The suffering she saw here in Ghana was similar but with its own particular characteristics. People met in the streets, exchanged news and went to buy goods in the near empty markets. The men tried to provide for their families and the women cared for the children. In the evenings she saw gleaming eyes and flashing teeth in the lamplight as she walked about. But beneath this apparent normality there was a tiredness and a wretchedness. No joyful children in these streets. Without enough to eat, although life continued, energy was missing.

The resilience that had so impressed her in Bangladesh seemed to be replaced here by resignation. So far the ActionFirst funded projects had not impressed her. They did not seem to be pushing for radical change. What they did was good, and no doubt very worthy, but too often she heard the phrases "it's god's will" and "god will provide" going unchallenged on people's lips. Wasn't the whole point of development work to get people to act to change their lives? to stimulate them into altering the status quo, not just let them passively accept it? Certainly that's what Martine always said, insisting that even god required a helping hand. The projects she'd visited in Dhaka had reflected that self belief and can-do attitude.

She was jolted out of her reverie by Nigel's voice, "That's Osubuso ahead, we'll be there in just a few minutes." He twisted round to address Imogen directly. "Fiona Tisdale is the project manager here, and if I know Fiona, she'll have laid on a welcome of some sort, singing and dancing. The Ghanaians love this sort of occasion and they're usually very colourful. It should be easy to get some good shots for general publicity purposes, if you're quick about it."

Imogen nodded, keeping her irritation to herself. If there was one thing she hated it was being told how to do her own job. Nigel had made similar suggestions to her several times, although she hadn't noticed him advising the two men in the same patronising way. She checked her equipment: cameras, zoom and close-up lenses, flash. These were where they always were in the camera bag that she wore like a second skin. Plenty of film too. The car was slowing down and Imogen reached forward to tap the driver on the shoulder.

"Let me out here, could you, Kwame? That way I'll be ready for the action. Thanks." She jumped lightly to the ground, allowed the car to pass her into the compound, and followed quickly. As she busied herself with her work Imogen was half regretful that she had not brought a video camera. The still shots probably wouldn't do justice to the light, movement and colour of this, and the addition of a soundtrack would be perfect. She grinned to herself contentedly, however, sure of her skills in capturing the scene before her.

About twenty people were lined up in a semi-circle in front of what appeared to be the main building. They were all in traditional cloth, men as well as women, and the colours were brilliant in the hazy sunshine. The dust was not winning here, at least, thought Imogen gratefully. The staff swayed rhythmically, clapping to the beat of the song. The phrase 'to make a joyful noise' came unbidden into Imogen's mind. It was something Miss Pinder, her primary school teacher used to say in their music lessons. "*Well, Miss P, it's a pity you never heard this lot. They know exactly what you meant.*"

The song over, a very black man stepped forward "Akwaaba," he began a short speech, using the Twi word for 'welcome' which Imogen now recognised. Only after he finished did Fiona herself move out of the line to greet the visitors. Imogen registered her as a solid woman of an indeterminate age between thirty and forty. She too wore a colourful outfit, a loose fitting top and slightly tapered trousers which ended a few inches above her ankles. Her hair was pulled back and coiled tightly at the back of her head. Her freckled face was open and friendly, but with a determined chin. She spoke in a low, rather melodious voice which Imogen found pleasant, although she was too busy with her camera to pay much attention to the words.

The welcome over, they were led on a tour of the project compound. Kofi Paul and Agnes, two more senior staff, introduced themselves and explained the use to which the various buildings were put, dealing confidently with questions. Once again, Imogen noticed, Fiona kept in the background and left the Ghanaians to take the lead. Maybe at last here was someone with an understanding of what development meant.

Agnes preceded the group into the last building. "This is usually the outpatients clinic," she was saying, "but at the moment we're using it as a malnutrition unit."

The building had several rooms and, from what Imogen could make out, most of them were occupied by at least three families. She put her camera to one side as she listened to Agnes. "In all there are nineteen children staying here at the moment. The youngest is about six months old and the oldest five years. We don't have any over five years staying because, as you can see, we are already very full. Usually the children and their mothers stay about four weeks. Then we discharge them with a small supply of food."

Imogen felt tears pricking at her eyes as she looked at the children in the room. Most were emaciated, their knobbly little bones clearly outlined through their skin. Their heads appeared too big, swollen out of proportion to the tiny bodies, when in fact the opposite was true. Their bodies were shrunken. One was picking desultorily at a scab on his leg but most were perfectly still, cradled in their mother's laps or lying on makeshift beds of cloth. A few were swollen up with some kind of additional disease, Imogen presumed, their skin flaky and peeling. One whimpered constantly. What difference was one month of food going to make to them? Imogen felt her hopes for the Osubuso project shrivel away before they had even begun. Another pathetic stop-gap, she raged inwardly. Why was nobody doing anything to stop this happening?

As if reading her mind Fiona added to Agnes' explanation. "It may seem that what we're doing here is a drop in the ocean when you consider the scale of the problem, but we have to be realistic. We only have space for a very small number of children here, and although we're privileged, even we don't have limitless food. We depend on the same markets as the general population, with some additional donated goods. So we're trying to spread our help as widely as possible, but so that it's still enough to make a difference." Fiona paused and took a notebook down from a shelf, running her finger rapidly down the page, her lips moving in a silent count. "So far we've had one hundred and fifty three children living here altogether. Each one has gone home between ten and twenty percent heavier than when they came in. We hope that's enough to enable them to survive until the rains finally come and new crops can be grown." She turned to another of the local staff. "Felicia, would you show our visitors the recipe book and explain how it works? Thanks."

Felicia told them how the recipes were devised together with the women, using their ideas along with the nutritional knowledge of the staff. They discussed the recipes with the agricultural staff too, trying to concentrate on foods which could be grown easily in the women's own gardens. Imogen tried to listen through her impatience, thinking that surely there must be more effective ways of addressing the problem than messing about with recipe books like a perverted version of the Women's Institute.

The tour completed, Fiona led the four visitors into her house for some refreshments and to go over their programme for the next few days.

"I'm sorry, but I was only expecting three of you," she said apologetically. "Nigel, your letter only mentioned yourself, Keith and Leo. I didn't know you were bringing anyone else." She glanced at the unknown woman with the cameras.

"This is Imogen Pollock. She's acting as official photographer on this trip." Nigel made the introductions. "She did some work for ActionFirst in Bangladesh, produced some very fine photos, and I thought it would be a good idea to bring her along. It was a bit of a last minute decision. I'm sorry we didn't let you know." Nigel's apology was minimal, his thoughts had quite clearly already moved on.

"Well, the thing is," Fiona paused, thinking quickly. She didn't want the poor woman to feel she was a nuisance, it obviously wasn't her fault, and it was typical of Nigel not to think anything of it. "The Presbyterian Guest House where I've booked you in, they only have one twin and one single room. I hope you don't mind, Imogen, but it looks like you'll have to stay here." *'And that's the last bloody thing I need'*, Fiona finished silently.

Nigel was already deep in conversation with Kofi Paul, Fiona noted, his long angular frame folded into the chair like a praying mantis. It seemed he had simply assumed she would have a solution, if he even realised there was a problem. She had met Nigel before, both back in the UK and not long after her arrival in Ghana. She found him a difficult man to work out. In the UK context he was efficient and sharply analytical. He maintained an old-fashioned courtesy but it never crossed the line into the patronising manner which he displayed so frequently during his overseas visits. She smiled quickly at Imogen who was looking distinctly uncomfortable. "It's basic but comfortable enough, I hope."

"I'm terribly sorry. I don't like to put you to any trouble. Are you sure there's nowhere else? I don't mind bunking in with one of them." Imogen did mind but she could see Fiona was angry at Nigel's lack of consideration. What an arrogant wanker he was, carrying on as if nothing was amiss.

"They wouldn't allow that up at the Presby!" This time Fiona's smile was genuine, lifting and lighting her face. "You don't know what a stickler Faustina is for propriety. She'd have a fit. As long as you don't mind me not being an attentive hostess, it'll be easiest if you stay here."

"OK. Thanks. I'll try not to get in your way." Imogen warmed to Fiona's ready sense of humour.

"Good. I'll get Esther to show you round, if that's OK. I'd better join the others."

Esther, Fiona's capable-looking middle aged 'house-girl' showed Imogen where to put her things in the spare bedroom, explained the bucket system for flushing the loo, showed her the filtered drinking water in the fridge, and asked how she liked her tea in the mornings. It was a compact little house but it had a comfy feel. The rectangular main room was spacious, with a large table, three armchairs, a desk and a small bookcase crammed with books. A short corridor led round a corner from one end of the room to the bathroom, with a bedroom off each side. The kitchen was through a door at the other end of the central room. A wide verandah stretched right across the back of the house. Imogen sat in one of the armchairs and completed her notes about the pictures she'd taken so far.

<u>3</u>

Fiona felt the tension in her neck and shoulders begin to work it's way over her scalp. This sort of discussion always had the same effect on her. It wasn't that she didn't understand the theoretical arguments, or find them interesting, just that her own focus was more pragmatic: what needed doing and how it could be done. Principles were all very well but there was always more than one way to achieve them.

"But economic sustainability is essential" Leo's face was set in angry determination. "There's no future unless people can hold their own economically. It's pointless to go on providing handouts, subsidising existence. It just goes nowhere."

Nigel shook his head wearily. "I know those arguments, Leo. You've made them often enough and I don't doubt your sincerity." Leo's face grew darker still. "However, ActionFirst is not driven by economics. It's driven by humanitarian principle and, as the name reminds us, the need to act. We cannot simply abandon people because they have not moved as fast in one direction as we hoped."

When Fiona caught Keith's eye, he gave her a sympathetic grimace but made no effort to try and intervene in the argument that had already been going on for several minutes. Fiona had the impression it was a recurring theme. The battle between the two men reflected a deeper struggle within the organisation, as in wider development circles, between the hard-nosed devotees of economic reform and those with a broader social development perspective.

"The public is becoming more critical, more sophisticated in their understanding of aid and development. If we don't respond to that pressure and begin to convince them that this is not just a bottomless pit of need, then donations will dry up altogether." Leo was on a roll. "I've seen the figures: donations are falling every year. Even the big charities are struggling to maintain their income from regular supporters. We've got to be much more realistic in the way we deal with development issues."

Nigel raised a hand. "That may well be true, but I dispute the overall trend," he interrupted. "Look at the success of organisations such as Comic Relief, or the other televised popular events: telethons, concerts and comedy shows. The level of public involvement is phenomenal. Donations have simply changed in nature, not dried up as you're trying to suggest. And what drives people to give is a sense of shared humanity, not some cold calculation about the interrelatedness of their economy with that of another country. And I think that's even more true since the US tragedy. People, even some in government positions, are beginning to realise that their own security depends on more equitable development. Look at all the promises to increase the aid and development budget."

"But without a firm economic foundation, there is nothing to develop with." Leo exploded. "OK, it's true that governments are talking about making a greater financial commitment, but when you read the small print, it's clear what sort of results they're looking for. It's about solid economic prosperity not simply feeling good."

"But solid economic prosperity depends on political stability, which in turn depends on people feeling a sense of security and hope. You can't get that through a business transaction. It takes investment in the people themselves, in their hopes and dreams as well as their houses and farms. And there's more than one way to skin this particular cat, Leo, as well you know." Nigel rushed on, anticipating Leo's interruption. "I spend a lot of time with donors. I know how they think, and yes, maybe there has been a change of emphasis among the big boys, but we have to appeal to the public too, and their focus has not changed. It is to alleviate the suffering of their fellow human beings."

"Well, then, tell me how that can be done without paying attention to the capacity of a country or an individual to earn an income so that they can purchase the goods and services they need. Without that, there is no progress." Leo stuck to his guns obstinately.

Fiona drew a deep breath. She couldn't take any more of this. "Look, I'm sorry to break up this discussion, but I really think we need to sort out the programme for the next few days." She smiled apologetically at the two men, feeling their antagonism shift in her direction. "There's obviously merit on both sides of the debate, and I think the real question is getting the right balance: economic development with a human face. Surely it doesn't have to be just one or the other."

Here she was rewarded by Keith's supporting comment of "Exactly." Encouraged by a slight decrease in the tension around the table, Fiona moved on. "We've put a lot of thought into your visit, and I'd like Kofi Paul to outline the plans we've made, now, if that's OK?"

Kofi Paul looked around the table, accepting Leo's shrug and Nigel's wave of a hand as permission to begin. "I think the programme we've put together will give you the opportunity to assess the economic strength of the project as well as the social impact," he began with a smile. Fiona let out a breath she hadn't realised she was holding: she could always rely on Kofi Paul to say the right thing. She allowed her mind to wander off, running through some of the duties she still needed to attend to after the meeting finished.

The tension in the room slowly ebbed away as the group focused on the detail of Kofi Paul's plan, and Fiona felt her shoulders relax and the imminent headache recede.

<u>4</u>

The next morning, the ActionFirst team set off to see the agricultural work which the project was undertaking. Kofi Paul informed them that this visit would not be to a single project farm, as they might have expected, but to a number of farms owned by local people. Given the drought, he explained further, what they saw might not impress them, but if they talked to the people they met, this would give them a better idea of what the project was doing.

The villagers were well prepared for the visit, Imogen quickly realised, impressed with Kofi Paul's quiet confidence. His relationships with the farmers were genuinely warm and it was clear they respected his judgement. But they were not subservient, freely expressing their doubts about some of his plans. The issue of the bush fires came up several times. Kofi Paul did not try to hide these disagreements, rather he made a slight joke of them, both with the visitors and the farmers themselves.

They saw a number of farms as they passed through the villages. The people Kofi Paul introduced them to included roughly equal numbers of men and women. Keith talked quietly with some of the women. It was his way of avoiding the running battle between Leo and Nigel; wherever he could he picked out the lower status people among those they met. He gathered a lot of useful information this way, much of it more honest than the 'official' line given to Nigel by the project or village bigwigs. This gave the team's eventual assessment a valuable realism and diversity of perspective.

Nigel, looking colonial in a khaki safari suit, responded to the obvious deference of the farmers by becoming all the more pompous. Leo seethed as he tried to wrest the limelight away for himself. "It would be laughable, really, if it wasn't so pathetic," Imogen muttered under her breath. Each of the men continually tried to engage their informants only on those issues of personal interest to them. Kofi Paul, especially, was subjected to intense pressure by both men. Imogen found it hard to concentrate on the camera work as she observed his reactions.

"So what steps are you taking to ensure that all farmers have a chance to benefit, and that indigenous knowledge is built on, not simply ignored?" That of course was Nigel. Kofi Paul responded with an explanation of the participatory processes employed in the agricultural work. Then Leo broke in with a question of his own.

"What about marketing, Kofi Paul? We're a long way from any significant population centre here. How do you ensure that produce can be sold at a competitive price?" Once again the response was readily made as Kofi Paul informed them of the links to both local and more distant markets. "It's certainly a challenge" he agreed. "At the moment we find it most effective to concentrate on small scale local markets, but we are exploring the possibility of creating wider cooperative networks through which the farmers can negotiate better terms for transport and sale. We'll be meeting some of those involved later."

Imogen turned away to hide her amusement. Kofi Paul was dealing with the two of them magnificently. Time and again he managed to find an answer which left neither on top. He'd missed his vocation. The diplomatic corps would be more appropriate.

Keith, having returned his attention to the main group, tried to steer the conversation onto neutral territory again. "I was interested in what you were saying about the idea of layering different crops in the one plot, Kofi Paul. Could you explain that to us a bit more?"

"Of course. It's known as permaculture. The principles are similar to those of crop rotation, but simpler, without the need to rotate anything. It's based on planting complimentary crops together, which place different demands on the soil." Kofi Paul began. Imogen's mind wandered off as the technicalities of the system were explained in some depth. She completed her official photos but continued to work, moving quietly between the men and women, capturing the essence of their farming work for her own use. Any fool could see the women made an essential contribution to the farms, she brooded. At least she could make sure her photography helped redress the view that farmers were always men.

Kofi Paul had arranged for them to eat in the last village and this was the occasion for some ceremony. Seats were brought out and arranged around a rickety table. A cloth was spread and plates, forks and spoons put upon it. This was done by two or three older women, assisted by young girls who did most of the running to and fro. Imogen took the opportunity to sketch some of them quickly in a pause in the official programme.

Nigel came into his element in these situations. He was indisputably the public leader of the party and it was to him the speeches were addressed. He also had the task of responding which he did at length but often to no particular point. His usual clarity of thought appeared to desert him on such occasions, and he waffled interminably on, using long words, impressive only if they were linked together by a theme. This Nigel hardly ever achieved. But the audience responded to his presence and the fact that his attention was on them. The detail of what he said escaped them, as their grasp of English was not enough to cope with the elaborate rhetoric. Kofi Paul acted as translator and Nigel appeared unconcerned that he was able to condense the long convoluted passages into so few words of Twi.

Once the speeches were done, the old women brought the food. It was groundnut soup with fish, accompanied by boiled rice. The soup was quite spicy which was to Imogen's taste. The fish, with heads and bones intact were not. She wondered briefly where all the food had come from, then realised that the project would have supplied most of the ingredients for such a formal occasion.

Ever alert to signs of gender injustice, Imogen became increasingly outraged during the drive back to Osubuso in the late afternoon. They passed many people walking home. The women, almost without exception carried heavy headloads of firewood, topped with whatever garden produce they could still collect from their depleted farms. Often they carried a child too, held onto their backs by a tightly wrapped cloth. By contrast many men carried only a single machete. Imogen reflected angrily that ActionFirst's projects did not seem to achieve any wider impact on this common division of labour, despite all the fine words on equity and progress.

<u>5</u>

"I'm expecting a disturbed night tonight," Fiona told Imogen after their late supper. "It's Patience on duty, and we've decided her name is spelt "p-a-t-i-e-n-t-s" because she always attracts them whenever she's on. I'll try not to disturb you, but if you do hear anything, that's what it will be."

"OK." Imogen nodded as she made her way through to the guest bedroom at the front of the house. "Thanks for the warning."

As usual Fiona awoke with the sound of the nightwatchman's feet on the path outside the door. She was half out of bed before he knocked: "Coming," she called softly in response to his summons. Her old operating theatre dresses were excellent for night calls, you just pulled them on and that was it. No buttons, belts, zips, no nothing.

She stepped off the porch and set off towards the maternity ward, only to hear Kwadjo's voice from the corner of the house. "No, Sister. This way. Come this way." He was waving an arm towards the hedge which surrounded the compound at the back of the house. Fiona was puzzled. Was it an accident? The house and maternity unit were about fifty yards apart at the top of the sloping compound. The outpatient building was lower down, adjacent to the road and the main entrance. A shorter but steeper path led up from the town behind the house and it was toward this Kwadjo was urging her. She moved quickly down the slope and turned the hedge corner. A woman was lying on the ground moaning slightly with Patience bent over her in attendance. There was a small bundle beside them.

"Sister, she's delivered already." Patience's voice was urgent. "Can you take the baby, it's not crying, I don't know ..."

"Is she alright? No bleeding?"

"Yes, she's fine. Everything is fine. The afterbirth's coming now. It's just the baby. Please."

Fiona took a quick look into the cloth bundle, resting her hand gently on the baby's chest. There was no perceptible sign of life and already the tiny limbs felt cool. Not a moment to lose. She scooped the bundle up and ran towards the ward, almost knocking Imogen down as she rounded the corner of the house. She had no time to explain or apologise.

In the ward she unwrapped the baby. It was a boy and a reasonable size. From what she'd seen, he couldn't be more than a few minutes old. She laid her stethoscope to his chest listening intently. Yes, definitely a heartbeat, but slow and faint. His colour was not good. She noticed Imogen standing with a shocked expression a little behind her and explained, "He hasn't cried, and he hasn't started breathing yet. I'll have to resuscitate him." She cleaned the baby's mouth quickly with a finger and then very gently blew into his chest, filling only her cheeks as she breathed into him. At the same time her hands kept up a constant massage, stimulating his seemingly lifeless limbs. To Imogen, watching motionless, it seemed an eternity passed. There was a sudden convulsion, the baby's chest heaved, then he cried. It was a feeble effort at first but he soon mastered the skill, and was yelling lustily when Patience came in, supporting his mother. From the pure joy on the woman's face Imogen knew she'd thought the baby was dead. It was a little while before Fiona could escape from her enthusiastic thanks.

Trying to keep control of her own emotions, Imogen looked around the ward. It was basic to say the least, iron beds with thin, foam mattresses and a dull grey cement floor. Beside each bed was a cot, but most of the babies were sleeping with their mothers on the beds. She counted nine women. The labour room was lit, if such a dim light counted, by a single, unshaded bulb. Imogen wondered idly why they didn't invest in brighter bulbs, not understanding that the problem lay in the electricity supply itself. The bed in the labour room was iron, too, but higher than the ones in the ward with a rubber covered mattress. In between the ward and the labour room there was a utility room with a sink. She registered a kerosine stove and a set of weighing scales among the less familiar items lining the shelves and table. The whole place looked as though it could do with some serious renovation and redecoration.

"Seven pounds and one ounce," Patience announced, lifting the baby from the scales. "Should I wash him, Sister Fiona? D'you want to get back to sleep?" All the staff knew the pleasure Fiona got from bathing the new babies, so even in the middle of the night, they checked before taking on the task themselves.

"No, Patience, I'll wash him. He's a bit special this one." She smiled at Patience whose expression was indulgent. Fiona filled the bath and lowered the soft little body into the water. She made sure the bath was deep enough for the water to cover the baby, keeping him warm and secure. This one was a strong little creature and now very alert. His dark eyes stared straight at her as she held his head steady in the water. She soaped his curly hair, feeling its springiness under her fingers as she picked out the dirt which was mixed into the half dried blood. As she washed his fingers they curled around her own with the lock-tight grip of the newborn. There was nothing quite like a brand new baby, she reflected, no matter how many she delivered each one gave her the same thrill. It was only as she was drying him, "aren't you a lovely boy, then? Yes, you are," that she noticed Imogen was still in the room.

"We woke you up. Sorry. Come and have a closer look. He's pretty gorgeous, isn't he?" Fiona held the baby up for inspection. "Aren't you, Kwabena, just a bit handsome?"

"I hadn't really even gone to sleep, so I wasn't woken, as such," Imogen reassured her. "Is that his name? Hello, little fellow." Imogen seemed a little subdued. She swung her camera round and out of the way as she came closer.

"Like any boy born on Tuesday, he'll be a Kwabena." Seeing Imogen's puzzlement, Fiona continued, "everyone has a name for the day of the week they're born on, one set for girls and one for boys. What day were you born?"

"Wednesday, I think. That explains why I keep hearing the same names over and over. Doesn't it get confusing?"

"Then you'll be Akua. It's a very simple system, but it does cause problems with the clinic registers. Most people have Christian names too, or nicknames, but that doesn't seem to help as they forget which name they've used each time they visit. It gets chaotic sometimes." Fiona laughed.

Imogen was impressed by the calm efficiency with which Fiona worked. "How did you know he was alive?" she asked, a lump in her throat. "It's amazing, what you did."

"Not really," Fiona shrugged off the admiration, as she had with Kwabena's mother. "It's just a matter of training, you know, like you knowing what film speed and exposure to select. There's no magic involved."

"Well, it seemed pretty special to me." Imogen grinned at her, recovering a little from the reverence Fiona's skills induced. "And even you can't deny that his mother thinks you're a miracle worker."

"Don't be daft." Fiona took the baby to his waiting mother as she spoke, once more waving her gratitude away. "I'm off back to bed now, Patience. I'll finish the notes properly in the morning. No more calls tonight, I beg you." This was said with a smile and the characteristic tap of the back of her right hand into the palm of her left in the pleading gesture seen throughout Ghana. Patience was busy re-sterilising the instruments. "Only three more times before morning, Sister, I promise," she joked back.

Fiona and Imogen walked back to the house together. "Did you get any good pictures, then?" Fiona asked. "I can't believe you thought to get a camera in the middle of the night."

"I'd just taken off my walkman when I heard you round the back of the house, so I got up to look. I grabbed the camera automatically. I might have got some good ones. I hope so."

"Well, hopefully it will be peaceful from now on. Sound sleep."

"Goodnight." Imogen went into the bedroom. She did not sleep immediately, replaying the scene she had witnessed in the ward over in her mind. Fiona was so absorbed in her work, so focused. Had she managed to capture that on film? The shots of the two of them during the baby's bath should be good. What she'd just witnessed was indeed a miracle, even if an everyday one to its performer. Still impressed, she turned over and drifted off to sleep.

6

In the morning Fiona yawned hugely as she sat down to breakfast. "Excuse me," she said. "I hope you weren't woken again?" Imogen shook her head. She'd slept like a log after the early interruption. "Good. I asked Kwadjo to come round and tap on my window instead of knocking at the door so as not to disturb you any more." She stretched. "We had another couple of babies in the night so we're full up. Typical of Patience. Thank goodness it's not her again tonight. One busy night is enough for me."

"Do you have to do a lot of night duty? It must be exhausting."

"The three of us share it, Agnes, Comfort Atta and me. There's always one of the nurse aides on night duty. They only call us when they need and it's not so often now they're more confident, usually just when a mother arrives and for the birth. We each do three nights in a row which means you get to recover in between times. And not every night is busy." She paused, lifting her spoon to take another mouthful of breakfast. "I hope rice pudding for breakfast is OK for you. At the moment there's not a lot else to eat."

Imogen nodded her head. "It's fine, I can eat it any time, not like Mary Jane." At Fiona's bewildered look she went on. "You know, from A A Milne: 'what is the matter with Mary Jane? She's perfectly well and she hasn't a pain. And it's lovely rice pudding for dinner again'. Didn't you read that as a child? I loved all of those poems."

Fiona's smile illuminated her face as she remembered, "Oh yes, of course, now I see what you mean." She laughed, no longer appearing as tired as at the start of the meal. Imogen carried on reminiscing. "There was King John who wasn't bad, and Sir Brian who was, and I still think the idea of being six forever and ever is a pretty good one." The conversation ticked happily along on the topic of other favourite childhood books, Fiona admitting a fondness for the "Famous Five", until the men appeared at the door.

The plan for the day was to visit the women's co-operative groups. Kofi was accompanying them. Imogen was pleased that Nigel was unexpectedly staying behind but felt sorry for Fiona, who should have had the day to herself. "I'd like to go through a few accounting things with you, Fiona. Just to make sure everything's ship-shape and Bristol fashion." Nigel's next remarks, Fiona realised, were directed at Leo, rather than her. "It's my responsibility to make sure all ActionFirst's money goes where we say it does. We can't afford any sloppy accounting now we have such a financial wizard in the team, can we?"

"Fine, Nigel." Fiona said pleasantly, swallowing her annoyance. "If you don't mind waiting a while until I sort the clinic and children out first." The inspection of accounts was due the following day, but she knew it was not worth fussing. Nigel had made other small, unexpected changes to the original plan. It seemed to reassure him of his status. She caught Imogen's eye as the others went out to the waiting vehicle and saw the understanding sympathy in her look. Fiona shrugged, raising her brows very slightly in resignation. "Have a nice day now, you-all," she called mockingly after them.

She kept Nigel waiting half an hour longer than was strictly necessary just to make her own point. It would take them well into the afternoon to get through all the books. With such an erratic power supply the project had not yet joined the computer literate world. She went to find Agnes. "I'm sorry, Agnes, but we'll have to leave visiting the hospital till tomorrow. Nigel's decided to look at the books today. I know you wanted to see Ama soon, but I can't see any way to fit it in today, not now." Fiona raised her hands in a gesture of helplessness.

Agnes was experienced in the erratic behaviour of the 'oberunis', Twi for white people, having worked in aid projects for many years. She smiled placidly at Fiona. "Don't worry, she'll still be there tomorrow. I can sort out the stock instead, ready for the Ministry order next week."

With the guests off the compound for the day, Fiona and Agnes had planned to travel to the nearest major town, Afafranto, about an hour's drive away. The week before they had referred a woman in obstructed labour to the hospital there. She'd had a caesarian operation but the baby had not survived. Fiona hoped that they would be able to get away soon. They always tried to visit the women they referred, especially in such circumstances.

She took a deep breath, stretched and released her shoulders and walked back into the house. "OK, Nigel, that's everything sorted out, I hope. Now, what did you want to look at first?"

By the end of the afternoon Fiona had a thumping headache. Working with figures was not her favourite among the many jobs she undertook on the project, but she could manage the comparatively straightforward accounts well enough. Apparently, so Nigel informed her, the accounts division of ActionFirst was pushing for all projects to use a particular system which she might find a little more complex as she would not be using the normal computerised version. Nigel took it into his head to try and teach her some of the basics. Fiona realised this desire was linked to his battle with Leo. Aggrieved that she was the one to suffer for it, she gritted her teeth as he talked on.

"No, no, my dear girl, not there." He pointed to a series of columns in quick succession. "This figure must be transferred over here, and then these two are added and taken up here, lastly you take the sum of this, minus the sum of that to reach the final total. It's quite straightforward really, it's just a matter of being logical." His self satisfied smirk added to her irritation. Fiona forced her mind to focus on the figures before her, blotting out his insistent voice and confusing explanations as she painstakingly worked the new system out for herself. She had the satisfaction of making Nigel admit that she seemed to understand it all very well, but the headache was a high price to pay.

She sat in the armchair and rested her head back against the cushion, eyes closed. Inwardly she sent up a prayer for an undisturbed night. She ought to be entertaining Imogen better, she knew, but she couldn't summon the energy for small talk.

"Is it bad?" Imogen's quiet question surprised her out of her state of suspended animation. "The headache, I mean." Fiona's eyes flicked open briefly, she nodded minimally so as not to make it worse. "Spending a day with that man is enough to give anyone a migraine," Imogen continued. "I've tried, and some of his ideas are really good, but he's so patronising. I get too frustrated. I find I just have to switch off."

Fiona felt rather than heard Imogen come closer. "I lived with someone who had bad migraines once," she was saying. "Would you like me to massage your head. It always seemed to help her." Her fingers began to knead rhythmically at Fiona's temples, pressing just hard enough. She worked in silence for several minutes gradually moving her hands over Fiona's forehead, scalp and finally around to the back of her neck.

"Is that better?" she asked as she finished, moving back to sit in her own chair.

"Wonderful. Did you have to stop so soon?" The tension had almost gone from Fiona's face. "No, really, that's made a huge difference. Thank you. Look, I can turn my head now without it falling off." She smiled for the first time since Nigel left.

Another few moments passed in a companionable silence, before Fiona spoke again. "I know what you mean about Nigel. I don't know what comes over him on these trips. He's not nearly so bad back in the UK office."

"He's positively embarrassing sometimes, coming the colonial over everyone." Imogen spoke with some force. "But what's pissing me off most is the ridiculous rivalry between him and Leo. They're behaving like children."

"It is a bit hard to take sometimes, I agree, but Keith says they've been at each other's throats since Leo was appointed. Nigel was the founding father of ActionFirst, you know, and underneath it all he is passionate about what we do. I think he finds Leo's one-track economics-is-king theme a bit hard to swallow, and it irritates him that he knows he has to accept that he's actually got a point, even a small one." Fiona felt a tinge of disloyalty discussing the others with Imogen, but it was good to have someone to talk to.

"Well, Leo is a bit single minded, I suppose, but at least he treats other people as if they've got a brain."

"On the surface, but I think it's Nigel who really listens. When all's said and done, Leo isn't going to change his mind, but I've seen Nigel admit to mistakes quite a few times. I've got a lot of respect for him, despite his being a patronising, pompous idiot sometimes." Fiona grinned.

Imogen reluctantly conceded that this might be true, but was unwilling to let Nigel off the hook altogether. She tossed her head, shaking her hair out of her eyes. "But that's what I mean, his attitude to women, it stinks. I don't think he even sees them unless they have a drink or food in their hands." Imogen paused. "Mind you, Leo's as bad most of the time. Keith's the only one with any sort of gender awareness. Why isn't there a woman on the team, anyway, I thought that was policy?"

"Nigel probably thinks you're doing very nicely in that capacity." Fiona laughed again. "I nearly strangled him this afternoon when he kept calling me his 'dear girl' and explaining that new accounting system as if I'm a simpleton. If he'd have just shut up I'd have cracked it much quicker. But on a more serious note, I know they've been struggling to replace the gender officer for the Africa programme since Mandy had to leave so unexpectedly. Normally she would have been here knocking a bit more sense into them and giving shape to Keith's efforts."

"Well, I don't know if I'll get through the rest of this trip without a murder on my hands." Imogen grumbled, not seeing the funny side at all. "Either that or he'll drive me to drink."

"Speaking of which I'm being a terribly neglectful hostess." Fiona stood up. "I've got some beer in the fridge, would you like one? I shouldn't as I'm on duty, but I need one after today. It would be nice if you'd join me."

Imogen needed no further invitation. The conversation moved on to other topics, although still related to the project. "Kofi Paul seems a very able man. I'm surprised he isn't in a more senior position." Imogen gave Fiona an inquiring look.

"I know, he should be." Fiona sighed. "I'm hoping that he'll be made project manager after I leave next year. I haven't had a chance to talk to Nigel yet, but I had a word with Keith about it. He's always influential in selecting staff. He's in favour except for the fact that it would mean employing an extra midwife, which could be a strain on the finances."

"But that's what ActionFirst's goal is, isn't it? To create a situation where people are in charge of their own development? At least that's what they all say, but no one seems to act on it much. They'll probably put in another expat." Imogen's tone was sarcastic and her flashing eyes and rigid posture expressed her disgust equally clearly. Fiona noted idly how easy it was to read the emotions of the woman opposite her. Her highly mobile features registered each passing thought. Her movements were quick and definite like her speech. Perhaps, mused Fiona, it was looking at the world through the lens of a camera which made her so quick to judge, to visualise everything in such oppositional terms.

"Perhaps it's not as simple as you think," she said a little wearily. "It's not just a matter of saying, 'there you are, get on with it'. Money is important, but you have to build up trust and confidence first."

"But that's so paternalistic. You sound just like Nigel! As if these people have no minds of their own. Surely you can't think that way?"

"No, I don't think that, at all." Fiona swallowed the last of her beer, mentally reminding herself of the time it had taken her to accept the slow pace of change. "Ghanaians are among the most educated people in west Africa. Many of them are very able, like Kofi Paul, Agnes and the others. But they don't necessarily agree with our sense of priorities. Why should they? They're more focused on daily life, the struggle to provide for their families, to protect the little they have against misfortunes like drought, or illness." She yawned.

"But surely the priority has to be to get things changed so that this sort of thing doesn't happen to them. To get people to take action to prevent it in the first place." Imogen did not feel drowsy at all. This was just the sort of conversation she missed from the men. "It just needs some forward thinking, planning, that's all."

But Fiona yawned again and, giving in to tiredness, said, "I'm sorry, but I have to get to bed. I need some sleep in case I'm called again." Seeing the disappointment in Imogen's face she went on, "I'm not giving you the brush off, Imogen, really, I'm done in. Can we save this for later, when I'm not on duty?"

Imogen was instantly contrite. "Yes, of course. I'd forgotten you were up most of the night. I'm sorry. I hope you get a better sleep tonight, but I'll hold you to that promise." She smiled up at Fiona, who stumbled off to bed, eyes already half shut. Imogen, her mind fired up by their brief debate, looked for distraction. The bookshelf drew her eye and she moved across to it hoping to understand more of Fiona by checking the kind of reading she did. She was reassured by what she found, picking carefully through the volumes before taking one off to bed.

7

On the evening of the final day of the ActionFirst visit, the team and the project staff gathered at Fiona's house. Normally she would have fed everyone, but this time she limited her hospitality to snacks and drinks. In the circumstances the staff had agreed that a fancy meal was inappropriate.

The atmosphere was upbeat. Even Nigel and Leo appeared to have called a temporary truce. The last day had been as successful as the first three, and Fiona felt that she and her staff had survived the ordeal well. She and Agnes even managed to sneak off to see Ama in the hospital, after all. This being a formal occasion, Nigel, of course, decided a speech was needed. Fiona exchanged a speaking look with Kofi Paul, groaning inwardly, '*not again!*' But for once Nigel was reasonably short and to the point.

"My dear Fiona, Kofi Paul, Kofi and all of your staff, I would just like to say a few words of appreciation." He hurrumphed loudly, before continuing. "As you know we are currently reviewing ActionFirst's programme in Ghana. We need to make some decisions in relation to future funding. As you will be aware, our watchword is sustainability. We believe in long term development but we also believe in the need for local people to take control of that development. Our job at ActionFirst is to facilitate this process, to enable and encourage. We do this by providing funding and then, as in this trip, ensuring that those people who are locally responsible for that funding spend it according to plan." His audience shuffled, this was as familiar as breathing to most of them. "I am pleased to say that we," Nigel indicated Leo and Keith with his arm, "have found this project to be a highly satisfactory one."

The local staff members interrupted with a burst of clapping, but Nigel still had more to say. "You have gone above and beyond the original brief of the project proposal in imaginative ways. The management of the project is exemplary." This with an avuncular nod in Fiona's direction. "The involvement of local staff in this management is also to be applauded. So, let me come to the point. Needless to say, there can be no decisions before we return and allow the full board to deliberate on our reports.

We must after all observe the proper formalities and due processes." Fiona could feel the Ghanaians holding their collective breath, and shared in their anticipation. "Get on with it, man," she muttered, causing Kofi Paul to give her an admonitory nudge in the ribs.

Nigel went on "That board meeting will take place in late May, nearly a month after we return to the UK. You will receive official confirmation of any decision only after that point. But I think I can speak for the whole team," Nigel looked once again at Leo and Keith for a positive reaction. They were well tuned to the rhythm of his speeches and knew their role despite not having paid attention to his words. Nigel beamed contentedly. "We will be recommending the continuation of our funding, pending decisions in a few key areas."

At this point Nigel was interrupted more seriously by the delighted cheers of everyone present. Fiona hugged the other staff in delight. After a moment Nigel managed to recapture their attention for a final word. "At this point, obviously we are not in a position to confirm or make promises, but I am hopeful, given ActionFirst's recognised ability in the fundraising business," here he preened himself a little, "that you will not only continue but expand your activities. So, may I finish by offering you all my congratulations and expressing my belief, indeed my fervent hope, that you will carry on the good work you do for many years to come."

The party became quite raucous, despite Nigel's attempts to instill caution. Fiona thanked Nigel for his positive assessment of their work. "It's really good for the staff to have such direct praise. It means a lot, that recognition of their hard work."

"And yours, my dear, and yours." Nigel beamed at her in his fatherly way, and for once Fiona didn't mind a bit. She took the opportunity to broach the subject of her successor. "You know my contract is up in just over a year, don't you, Nigel?"

"There's no need to worry about that, my dear," Nigel interrupted, jumping to his own conclusions about where she was heading. "You've proved yourself to be more than able. We don't like to lose staff of your calibre. I'm sure an extension could easily be arranged." He laid a hand on her shoulder with a reassuring squeeze.

"No, it's not that. I'm not fishing for an extension," Fiona shook her head vigorously, managing to wriggle out of his grasp at the same time. "It's right that I should finish here. I think the local staff are more than ready to take over full responsibility."

"Well," Nigel looked thoughtful. "That sounds like you have a plan, young lady. I think the others need to be part of any discussion of the future."

To prevent this from stopping the discussion then and there, Fiona quickly caught the attention of both Leo and Keith, taking all three men out to the slightly quieter space of the rear verandah. She explained her proposition, emphasising Kofi Paul's readiness for the role, and drawing on Keith's support. "And if we don't give him this sort of opportunity ourselves, he's going to be snapped up by somebody else," she finished, slightly stretching the truth as she knew Kofi Paul did not want to leave Osubuso.

"It seems sound to me, except for the matter of the cost of employing a third midwife in addition to a manager. You've been excellent for the bottom line, Fiona," said Leo, catching her off-guard with this rare humour. "I was certainly impressed with his abilities when he came on the training course and my high opinion has only been strengthened by this visit. I'd be in favour as long as the costs can be borne by the project without negative effects in other areas."

Nigel, who had been listening thoughtfully to the discussion, spoke again. "Work up a proposal for me giving justifications and risks, you know, the usual format. If you can make a convincing case on the financial side then I'll put it before the board along with our recommendations. At this point it sounds a sensible proposition, but we need to go through all the proper procedures. It's an important decision."

Fiona thanked them and promised to have the proposal on Nigel's desk as soon as she could. They moved back inside to rejoin the party which was beginning to wind down. Agnes and Kofi came to say their goodbyes, setting off a general drift towards the door. Leo, Keith and Nigel were last to depart, and as usual Nigel had the final word. "We've got a long day tomorrow, Imogen, it's several hours drive up to Bolgatanga. We have to make an early start. Could you make sure you're ready to go by seven thirty, please." He paused with another smirk, "I wanted to warn you, not just show up. I know how long you girls need to get ready." Laughing happily he sauntered off into the night, leaving Imogen helpless with indignation.

"There! You see? I was about to allow myself to be generous about him and look what he says." Imogen's face was a picture. "I bet I get through a bathroom quicker than him any day."

"I'm sure you do." Fiona took the last beer from the fridge. "Go halves with me?"

"Sure." Imogen was still fuming over Nigel's last remark. "How dare he make assumptions like that? He takes all the prizes for male chauvinist pig, really. He's just impossible." She took the glass from Fiona's hand. They both jumped as a small electric shock passed between them.

"Ow! I better watch it, now even you're attacking me." Imogen grinned and took a slug of beer, sitting down with a sigh. "I s'pose you'll start defending him again, being as it seems he's doing the right thing by the project."

"No, not this time." Fiona's expression was gleeful, "although I'm even more pleased than you know. I've just got him to agree to Kofi Paul replacing me as manager, so long as I can write a convincing enough proposal for the board. I feel I could fly, I'm so pleased."

Indeed she was glowing, Imogen noticed, her gaze picking out the flush in Fiona's freckled cheeks and the sparkle to her green eyes. She was a most attractive woman in this mood. Imogen continued her assessment realising that under the rather shapeless clothes Fiona wore was a much more delightfully feminine body. She pushed the thoughts away, '*stop it, you're leaving tomorrow*' and, giving herself a mental shake, she focused on what Fiona was saying.

"Not long after I first got here I went through a spell of real depression. I didn't seem able to get anything started and there was so much to do. I'd suggest all sorts of things in the staff meetings, and everyone would agree but nothing ever got done. I was so frustrated I almost gave up. If it wasn't for Kofi Paul I think I would have done. He was the only one who really talked to me in those early days. He taught me a lot about development in general and these people in particular. If he becomes project manager, then I'll feel that I've repaid him just a little."

"What do you mean about the staff not acting on ideas?" Imogen was sure she must have missed something. "Your staff are among the most able I've come across and this project is bursting with activity."

"Yes, it is, now." Fiona emphasised the last word. "But it wasn't easy to achieve, to get them to believe in their own potential."

"I don't understand."

"Well, you were asking last night about why nobody did anything radical?" Imogen nodded, not quite seeing the connection, and Fiona carried on. "It took me a while to get over that same frustration. But Kofi Paul made me think about it from the point of view of local people, to understand that radical usually means risky."

Imogen interrupted her, "Yes, of course, but you have to take risks, or nothing changes. You have to have action, you have to force people to shift, to bring about a new balance of power."

"Easy for us to say, isn't it?" Fiona regarded her quizzically. "But it's not so easy to do, especially when you're already living life at the edge, no spare capacity to recover if things go wrong. Tell me, when was the last time you took some radical action?"

Imogen thought back, "Well, I was involved in the anti-debt campaign, we chained ourselves to the railings outside the bank." She saw the humour in Fiona's face, and reacted a little angrily. "It was pouring with rain. We were there the whole day, and we made the evening news bulletin."

"But apart from getting wet through, what did you suffer, a cold, perhaps? And I bet you had a warm house to go back to, even friends bringing you hot coffee and doughnuts."

"I do more than that. I write letters to my MP, and to lots of other officials overseas for Amnesty. I raise money. I talk to people. I do whatever I think will help."

Fiona smiled, "I'm sure you do, but it doesn't really affect your everyday life, does it?" She paused, finishing off her beer. Imogen looked both upset and puzzled. She certainly wasn't used to people telling her that she was not sufficiently committed to her beliefs. "Would you be so happy to act if it meant you might lose the respect of your family and friends? Or your income, especially if other members of a family depended on you?"

Imogen replied in an irritated tone, "What's that got to do with it? I put a lot of effort into persuading people to agree, and it bothers me when I can't, but how could supporting Oxfam or Amnesty lead to my financial ruin? That's just ridiculous."

"Of course it is, to you, but what about to people in other countries? Some of them need the help of organisations like Amnesty simply because they've been trying to persuade others to see their point of view, as you described it. That's what I mean when I say we live a very cushioned life in the UK."

"OK, OK, I take that point, but where's the connection to people here being so resistant to change? Here, in Ghana, there's no real fear of that sort of oppressive reaction, and I've heard people having very heated political discussions, so I still don't see that you've explained anything." Imogen was warming to the debate. "And we're talking about practical improvements here, better health, more food. Surely people want that?"

"Oh, yes, they want it alright. It's more a question of what price they're willing to pay to get it." Fiona took a breath, and Imogen leapt in again. "But there's no price, that's what I'm saying. Just a better life. How can it be so hard to do?"

"Oh, Imogen, if only it was that simple." Fiona's smile was a little weary. "But there's always a price to pay somehow, for someone. And the point I'm trying to make is that the people here can't afford it. They don't have much room to manoeuvre. You've seen how hard they work on their farms, and yet, just because the rains are a few weeks late, all that effort could be entirely wasted."

"But you're not listening at all. If they would take the risk of following some of Kofi Paul's excellent advice, not much of a risk at all, if you ask me, then they'd be better off. They'd grow more, have enough to eat, maybe even some to sell. Things would start to get better, instead of going round and round in this dreary cycle of never-ending poverty. What are you doing here, if you don't believe in changing things?" Imogen's eyes flashed a fierce challenge.

"I'm not explaining what I mean very well, am I?" Fiona said ruefully. "It's just that there's so much more at stake, and even Kofi Paul's ideas wouldn't protect them from a drought like this. It's about seeing things from a completely different perspective.

We're asking them to change the habits of generations, tried and trusted, even if not always successful. Besides, there's a whole pattern of social support that goes with the system they know, ways of managing in the bad times. Networks of solidarity stretching back over years. Nobody wants to risk losing that without knowing just what will replace it. It's a slow and careful business persuading them to try, and keeping the risks at a level they find acceptable." Fiona paused for a moment as she tried to think of a way to convince Imogen of the need for caution. "It's not about giving up on progress, or not wanting change. It's about the mechanism to achieve it, about not throwing the baby out with the bath water. Our pattern of life and level of development didn't come about overnight, it took centuries. We can't expect other people to do it so quickly."

"But the project's been here for nearly three years already. How long do people need to make up their minds, for goodness sake? If I was living here I'd be jumping at the chances you all provide for them." Imogen's hands waved excitedly to emphasise her words.

"Maybe it is to do with time. You know how the Ghanaians are always saying we have the clocks but they have the time? Well, they work to a timescale that's different, maybe twenty, or even fifty years. Certainly not the three year project cycle we're accustomed to. If there's one thing this job has taught me, it's patience, and just what an elastic word that can be. But I can see I'm not convincing you. Don't let's fall out over it. You stick to your principles and don't listen to a tired old pragmatist like me." Fiona finished with a wry look, remembering her own reluctance to listen to Kofi Paul's different brand of rationality.

Imogen, full of frustration because she could not grasp what Fiona was getting at, yet not wanting to appear rude by pursuing the argument, reluctantly moved the conversation in a new direction. "What made you come out here, anyway, and what were you doing before that?"

"I worked as a community midwife for years, and I was involved in a community development project working with low income families, trying to provide support in a more coherent way. That project came to an end at about the same time that I saw this advertised. I didn't want to return to just being a midwife again, so it seemed like a logical step. I needed a new challenge to get my teeth into." Fiona answered, not mentioning the romantic disaster that had provided an important additional force. "What about you? Nigel mentioned you'd been in Bangladesh, what made you go?"

"My lover, if I'm honest." Imogen quipped before answering more seriously. "I'd been involved with a lot of development issues at home, like I said, through a variety of organisations and groups. My friends will tell you I'm a terrible one for causes. So it seemed like a straightforward step, to go and see some of the work for myself. It was pure chance, the way the job came up, not my doing really."

Fiona enjoyed watching Imogen's face while she talked, fascinated by the ever-changing expressions. This gave her an apparent youth, a vitality, which was belied by the fine wrinkles around her eyes. She was probably in her early thirties, Fiona guessed. "What happened?"

"Martine, you probably know of her, she's ActionFirst's gender specialist for southeast Asia. She and I were an item at the time. She was going on a trip and offered me the place as official photographer. Against all equal ops policies, I know, but I jumped at it."

Fiona noted the more personal information Imogen provided without comment or surprise. "I remember Mandy spoke highly of Martine's impact on ActionFirst. I think they joined up about the same time. What did you make of Bangladesh?"

"It was the first time I'd been in a developing country, so lots of things struck me. But it was the floods that were most dramatic and appalling. There were such contrasts." Imogen's eyes unfocused as she thought back. "We visited one project right in the middle of the flooded area, an income generation thing for women. They were surrounded by indescribably stinking water, wading through it waist deep on a daily basis, but the work they did was the most astoundingly beautiful embroidery I've ever seen. Really delicate and detailed, and such vivid colours. Apart from anything else, I don't know how they kept everything so clean in the middle of such filth."

"Sounds fascinating. Is it really as crowded as people say?"

"Oh yes, hordes of people everywhere, all of them milling

39

about in seeming chaos, but things get done. Even in the middle of the floods, life went on. It was a real experience."

"Are you still involved with Martine?" The question was more personal than Fiona intended, but it just popped out.

"No, we split up not long after that." Imogen grabbed the chance. "You've been out here a long time. Don't you ever get lonely?"

"Oh, no. There's always too much to do to be lonely. Sometimes I wish I had my old friends around, yes, but the others are good company, and I've got to know a couple in Accra. I visit them every two or three months if I can."

"No one special then?" Imogen looked at Fiona directly, who found herself giving a surprisingly honest answer. "No, I'm not involved with anyone just now. I sort of swore off relationships before I came out here."

"It's a shame Kofi Paul's married, you get on really well with him." Imogen tried again, more blatantly to get at the information she wanted.

"Yes, I do, he's lovely, so's his wife, Victoria. She's the assistant head at the secondary school here." Fiona smiled into her eyes. "Maybe if I found an Afia Pauline then I'd be tempted." She laughed as Imogen blushed. "God help you if you ever play poker, Imogen, you can't hide what you're thinking at all."

"Well," Imogen blustered, "I just wanted to be sure. It's nice to feel there's a little solidarity around. It hasn't been easy spending all this time in entirely male company, you know." Her comment brought the conversation back to its starting point, and they digressed into another rambling analysis of the three men's personalities.

"Hey, look at the time," Fiona exclaimed. "It's gone midnight and you've got to be up early tomorrow. We'd better get some sleep." She paused, suddenly shy. "I'll see you in the morning, but it may be a bit rushed. I just want to say it's been a pleasure having you stay. I've really enjoyed your company. Thanks."

"Me too,"

"Sound sleep."

"Goodnight."

8

Fiona woke, suddenly alert in the dark room. She listened. There it was again, a low groan. She located the source of the noise as the bathroom and went to investigate. There was a louder moan as she got to the door, which was slightly ajar. "Oooh, help, please, somebody help." It was Imogen.

Fiona pushed open the door, taking in the scene in one professional sweep of her eyes. Imogen was hunched on the loo, one hand holding her stomach, the other to her head, bent almost double. Sweat stood out against her brow and her tanned olive skin had developed a ghastly greenish tinge.

"I think I'm going to be sick."

Fiona grabbed a bowl and held it for her, resting her other hand comfortingly between Imogen's shoulders as she retched. After a few moments Fiona handed her a damp flannel. "Here, this'll make you feel a bit better. You poor thing. Have you been up before this?"

Imogen shook her head miserably. "No. I'm sorry, I was trying not to wake you, but I didn't know what to do. It felt like both ends at once." She shivered violently as an attempt at a smile flicked over her drawn features.

Fiona reassured her, "Don't worry. I know how you feel, it's horrible." She was cleaning the used bowl as she spoke, her manner unflustered. Imogen did not look at all well.

"I'm cold." Imogen was shivering uncontrollably.

"You feel cold, but I think you've probably got a temperature. Do you think that's it for the moment?" Imogen nodded uncertainly, the spasms seemed to have passed. "Let's get you back to bed, then."

"I'm all wobbly." Imogen sounded surprised by this discovery, holding Fiona as she tried to walk across the room. Fiona's arm went round her waist, secure and supportive. In the bedroom Imogen sat down abruptly on the bed, her legs giving way. Suddenly aware of her semi-nakedness she pulled her T-shirt down to cover her goosebumped thighs. "I must be an awful sight," she mumbled.

Fiona smoothed the sheet, then bent to ease Imogen's legs round onto the bed. "I've seen worse, don't worry," she smiled.

She sat on the edge of the bed and waited for the thermometer to register, then regarded Imogen seriously. "Your temperature's really quite high. Tell me, have you been taking your anti-malarials?"

"They gave me such awful nausea," Imogen said, shamefaced. She closed her eyes, feeling wretched. "I stopped after two or three days. I didn't think I'd been bitten at all. Nigel said the mosquitoes wouldn't be bad with the drought. I thought ..." A tear trickled from the corner of one eye and ran down into her ear.

"You idiot," but Fiona's voice was soft rather than scolding. There was no point adding to Imogen's misery. "I think you've probably got malaria, then. If I get you some chloroquine tablets, d'you think you can manage to get them down with a bit of water?"

"I'll try."

"OK, I'll be back in a minute."

With an effort Imogen swallowed the tablets, grimacing anew at their bitter taste. "I don't know if they'll stay down. What if I'm sick again?"

"Let's just wait and see, shall we? If they do come up, I can always give you an injection instead, but I'd rather not." Fiona's matter of factness was soothing and Imogen relaxed a little.

"I feel so pathetic, and stupid," she muttered. A thought hit her. "How am I going to manage the trip to Bolgatanga? I can't bear the thought of bouncing around in the car, I already feel like I've been run over by a steamroller. I don't even have strength to sit up." There was panic in her voice, and again Fiona consoled her.

"That one's easy. You're not going."

"But what about . . . ? What will Nigel say . . . ?"

"Bugger Nigel. I'll deal with him. You're in no fit state to travel anywhere." Fiona reached forward her hand, smoothing Imogen's dark hair back from her damp forehead with a gentle movement. "Stop worrying. I'll explain to the others, they'll understand. You get some sleep now. I'm just across the hall if you need me, OK?" Imogen's eyes closed obediently.

There was not much point in going back to bed. It was already after five o'clock. Fiona made a cup of tea and sat on the verandah watching the day break. It was the one effect of the harmattan season that she loved, the cool, almost misty quality of the early morning air, the gentleness of the light. It was the nearest thing to an autumn morning that Ghana had to offer, and she was truly thankful for the brief respite from the tropical heat. As soon as the sun broke free of the horizon, the air would begin to burn under its scorching power and the magical freshness would be gone.

Fiona sighed deeply. How much longer till the rains finally came? They needed to replenish their barrels again today and the stream was in danger of drying up. Just when would the dark clouds to the south move in their direction and deliver relief?

At just after seven fifteen, Nigel, Leo and Keith rolled up in the Landrover. Nigel jumped out briskly and came over to the door where Fiona stood waiting. "Morning, is Imogen ready? We're a bit early but the sooner we get off the better."

"She's not well. I don't think she should come with you."

"Oh-hoh, feeling a little the worse for wear, is she?" Nigel smirked. "I thought she might have trouble this morning, the way she was happily knocking back the beer last night, but a hangover will soon wear off. I've got a spare pair of shades, if she wants them." He was clearly amused, not registering the seriousness on Fiona's face.

"She's got malaria, Nigel, not a hangover. I can't believe you let her think the danger was insignificant just because of the drought." Fiona spoke crisply. "She's in no condition to travel. She needs to rest for at least three days, until she finishes the treatment. And that's providing there are no complications."

Nigel for once seemed at a loss for words."Oh. Umm. Well." He scratched his head. "Well, I suppose we must be guided by you, you're the clinician after all." He paused again. "It's going to muck up our schedule very badly, though, being delayed so long."

"You don't need to be delayed. Just go ahead and Imogen can stay here. You'll be passing the door, virtually, on your way back down, so you can pick her up again then."

Nigel brightened, but was still a little doubtful. "Of course, that's a possibility, but there were some particular shots I wanted her to get." He saw Fiona's face darken and thought better of what he'd been about to say. "We'll manage, I'm sure. I think

Keith's brought his camera along. Yes, that will be fine. We'll call in for lunch when we pick her up on Tuesday, then?" He was back in the car and away before Fiona recovered from his blatant cheek.

'*So much for my long weekend off*' Fiona thought grumpily as she went back into the house, but she soon recovered her more positive mood. Although she could not travel to Accra as she'd half planned, she still had the next four days to herself. And once Imogen recovered it would be nice to have her company for a while longer.

9

At midday she knocked softly on Imogen's door, entering in response to the drowsy "come in".

"I've brought your next dose. How are you feeling now?" She handed Imogen the tablets and water. Imogen struggled up onto an elbow, took the glass and swallowed the medicine before replying.

"Well, I haven't been sick, but I still feel dreadful. All shaky, like really bad flu and my head's still thumping." She lay back against the pillow. "I'm just so tired. I can't seem to keep my eyes open." Her face was still pale highlighting the length and thickness of the eyelashes lying against her cheeks.

"Well, that's probably best," Fiona said. "You just sleep, but if you can, remember to have a little drink every time you do wake. I don't want you getting dehydrated." She left Imogen to doze and took the opportunity to spend the rest of the day writing the letters she owed.

The following morning Fiona took a slice of toast and a boiled egg in to Imogen for breakfast. "Here you are, I've raided the freezer for the last loaf to tempt you into eating. I always want boiled egg and soldiers when I'm poorly. I thought you might appreciate it too."

Imogen sat up, still finding it an obvious effort. "Thank you. You shouldn't be going to all this trouble for me, really."

"It's no trouble. I'm off-duty this weekend and so is Esther. It's nice to have someone to cook for." Fiona noted the crumpled bedsheets and Imogen's wrinkled T-shirt. When Imogen had finished eating, managing only half the toast, Fiona said, "You look pretty hot and sticky. What about a wash?"

Imogen looked doubtful. "It would be lovely, but I don't think I've quite got the energy to struggle with the buckets and all, just yet."

"It'll make you feel loads better, get rid of the stickiness. Come on," Fiona insisted. "I'll help you."

Imogen looked even more doubtful at this idea and Fiona laughed. "Don't be so prudish. I'm a midwife, remember? I spend most of my life dealing with women's bodies. There's no need to be shy."

"It would be nice to be clean," Imogen said wistfully, then making her decision. "OK, if you're sure, then it would be very nice."

"That's better. Just let me get the bathroom organised and then we'll get to it." Imogen heard Fiona moving about between the kitchen and bathroom, the sound of the kettle boiling, then water splashing into a basin. Fiona came back into the bedroom. "All ready for you now ma'am, if you'll just step this way." She had a towel folded over her arm and bowed with a little flourish. Imogen giggled weakly.

The humour broke the slight tension. Fiona guided a still unsteady Imogen into the bathroom, instructed her to sit on the plastic stool which stood in the corner under the useless shower head, and helped to ease her T-shirt over her head. She then helped her wash thoroughly from head to toe. Her touch was considerate, neither becoming too intimate nor too rough and impersonal. It reminded Imogen of being bathed by her mother as a child, and the slight remnant of embarrassment she felt disappeared altogether. The hot water felt glorious on her still tender skin, and some of the dreadful tiredness seemed to lift from her limbs.

Fiona wrapped her in a large towel and rubbed her dry. "Just sit there a minute, while I sort out your bed." Then Imogen was being helped back between deliciously fresh, crisp sheets. She sighed in contentment.

"Thank you. That's absolutely fabulous. I feel like a new born baby." She grinned as she realised the humour of what she said. "No wonder they enjoy their first baths with you so much."

"After the soft soap, the unpalatable truth," Fiona smiled, handing Imogen more chloroquine tablets as she spoke. "Only one more lot, tomorrow morning, so don't look so miserable," she chided, adding, "I've got to pop into town this morning, so I'll be away an hour or two. I don't want you getting up and about till after I get back. Understood?"

"I hear and obey," Imogen replied mockingly. It would be no hardship and she was pleased to hear Fiona was going out and getting on with things. It made her feel less of a burden.

By the evening Imogen was feeling considerably better. A delicious aroma tempted her out to join Fiona at the supper table. She felt a pang as she realised she'd hardly eaten for almost forty eight hours. "It smells great, what have you been making?"

"Kontomire egg stew," Fiona replied. "It's one of my favourites, and very nourishing. You need a bit of building up again, after a bout of malaria." She placed a steaming bowl on the table, filled with the appetising looking stew. Next to it she put a dish of boiled rice. "It's best with yam, but rice will have to do for now. There hasn't been any yam in the market for more than a month."

Imogen helped herself to a modest portion, although hungry her stomach still felt a bit fragile, and she didn't want to jeopardise her recovery. "Mmmm, it's lovely. How d'you make it? What's kontomire?"

"The leaf of the taro plant, it's a bit like spinach. Basically it's just scrambled eggs with boiled kontomire in, but there are a few secret spices to give it more zest, and you beat the kontomire into a puree to get the consistency right. I often put fish in too, but I left it at just the eggs this time. It's not too hot for you?"

Imogen shook her head. "No, I love spicy food, that's been one of the pleasures of this trip. All those road-side places, chop-bars, is it, you call them?" She ate steadily until her plate was empty, shaking her head at Fiona's offer of more.

"But you'll have some pudding?" Fiona grinned at her surprise. "Oh yes, we can run to pudding at the weekends, life has to have some luxury even in a drought." She went into the kitchen and returned with a bowl. "It's more nursery food, really. You'll probably think I'm regressing out here by myself, but it's hard to be inventive with evaporated milk."

"Milk jelly." Imogen exclaimed. "I haven't had that in years. I didn't think anybody made it any more. What flavour is it?"

"Raspberry. Is that alright for you?"

"Fine, yes." Once again Imogen concentrated on the food. She scraped the bowl thoroughly, as she always did with puddings, as if she might never get to eat another in her life. Fiona watched her in amusement. "You can have a second helping, you know, it's not rationed."

Imogen laughed. "I'm sorry, it's a terrible habit. I only just stopped myself from licking it clean. But thank you, I've had plenty. Save the rest for tomorrow, or have it yourself."

They spent the remainder of the evening sitting in the armchairs, Fiona reading a book and Imogen idly doodling on a sketch pad. Just after nine she said, "I'm off to bed, Fiona. I can't stay vertical any longer. See you in the morning."

"Yes. You should be fine now, the chloroquine seems to have done its job, but don't hesitate to wake me if you feel suddenly worse again. Malaria can be a bit tricky. Sound sleep."

<u>10</u>

Imogen's recovery was uninterrupted and by Sunday afternoon she was almost back to her old self. She took her sketch pad and pencils down to the malnutrition ward. She'd been itching to draw the children and the women looking after them, and was pleased to be given a second chance. She hadn't felt the camera was the right tool to capture their plight. The women were intensely interested in what she was doing, coming to check on her work regularly and discussing it among themselves. Usually it was children who surrounded her at such times, but these kids did not have the energy. While photography provided her bread and butter work, Imogen's real love was for sculpture. She used clay as her main medium, drawing on her sketches as a base.

Her concentration was complete and she lost all track of time. It was almost dusk when Fiona came to find her. "So this is where you've been hiding. What are you doing?" Seeing the sketch pad, she asked, "Can I see? I didn't realise you drew as well." Imogen handed over the pad which now had dozens of images filling its pages. "Fiona was silent as she leafed through it. She looked at Imogen with admiration. "These are excellent, so lifelike, and you've caught them really well. They're special." She handed the pad back. They walked over to the house together.

As they finished supper the power went off. Used to these sudden failures Fiona quickly brought out and lit a couple of kerosine lamps. These filled the room with a soft, yellow light which Imogen found made the room cosier, more intimate. "Do you get cuts often? I haven't noticed them before," she asked.

"Probably one or two a week, but often they're in the day time and not troublesome at all. It's difficult to meet the demand for power at the best of times, and the drought's really affected a lot of the hydro stations badly. I quite like the cuts, though, everything goes quiet."

And Imogen noticed that the noise from the town had become muted, just distant voices floating on the air. She became aware of the varied buzzing and chirruping of insects and the strange croak- singing of the frogs in the storm drains down by the road. These sounds were no longer obscured by electricity-dependent noise. "Oh yes. No more reggae or high-life. But what about if you get a mother coming in, how do you manage?"

"We do have a generator if we need it, but very often the lamps are enough with the normal deliveries. The generator's a bit of a pig to start. It's a crank handle like they used to have on cars. If it catches first time, I'm fine, but if I have to wind it more than once I end up feeling quite dizzy with the effort. And it's very noisy so it means everyone wakes up."

"You're so capable," Imogen said enviously. "I wouldn't know the first thing about generators or kerosine lamps. The people must really appreciate you too, the way you look after everyone so well, me included." She finished with a wry smile. "It makes me feel my little contribution to the developing world is pretty insignificant compared with the real work you do, day in and day out."

"In many ways I get much more from the people here than I give them. I'm learning all the time."

"Yes, but you are making a real difference in their lives. That's what I'm always saying back home, that I want to make a difference. That's why I got involved with ActionFirst, but what am I doing? Taking a few pretty pictures."

"That's too harsh," Fiona disagreed. "The work we do depends on money and the money only gets here because of the publicity. Your 'pretty pictures' as you dismissively call them, are what brings in the money. Without them there'd be no work at all."

"But anyone can point a camera and take a picture of a starving child, or a flooded house. They're ten a penny back home."

"Yes, and a lot of them show nothing else, I agree with you there. I get very angry with a lot of the publicity around fundraising when it emphasises helplessness, makes it appear that people just sit around doing nothing, when in reality they put every ounce of energy they have into the struggle for survival. No wonder we get 'compassion fatigue' if that's the impression people have."

"So you do think what I do is useless, in fact worse than useless. You think I'm distorting the truth and belittling these people." Imogen sank lower into her chair, depression settling on her features.

"No. I wasn't meaning you, personally, I was speaking generally about the quality of the stuff I've seen. What you produce is different, if those sketches are anything to go by. You give people dignity, you show that they are human, that they are surviving against the odds. Your images are just the sort we need." She saw that Imogen was not convinced and carried on, "You've got real talent, Imogen, and it shines through in your pictures. You're no voyeur, and what you do does make a difference."

"You really think so? You're not just saying that to cheer me up?"

"I really, honestly think so. I'm sure that's what Nigel saw in your work too. He's no slouch when it comes to judging which images he wants associated with ActionFirst. He'll only have the best, and that means the most truthful." Fiona stated firmly.

Imogen cheered up at last. "Well, that's what I try to do, and I suppose I do believe it makes a difference myself, or I wouldn't bother."

"Do you like the photographic work or the sketching best?"

"It's hard to say. I use them differently, you see. What I really like is sculpting. That's why I need the sketches. Photos can be a bit flat, two-dimensional. I usually work from sketches when I'm doing a clay piece."

"I often wish I could draw, especially here, but I'm a complete wash-out. Even stick figures are too difficult for me." Fiona lamented. "I'm a completely talent free zone, can't sing or dance either."

11

On Monday it was back to rice pudding for breakfast. Fiona pointedly placed some malaria prophylaxis tablets in front of Imogen. "If you take them with food, they shouldn't give you too much trouble, so please, no more messing about."

Imogen took the tablets with a grimace. Her brush with malaria made her curious about the disease. "Do the local people suffer badly from it?"

"It's one of the biggest killers, but it affects the children worst, like most things. By the time they reach adulthood, so long as they do, most people have developed a sort of uneasy truce with the disease." Fiona was thoughtful. "I've only had it once, but it made me think about the way the health service works here. Imagine walking two hours to reach the clinic the way you felt on Friday. That's why we started up the volunteer health posts to encourage sensible self treatment, although we still have a bit of a battle with people who think an injection's the only real cure."

"I'd have been hard pushed to get to the clinic just from the house," Imogen responded. "Now that I think about it, I'm amazed you get anyone in the clinic at all. I wouldn't be at all surprised if they all just curled up at home and said 'sod it'."

"Now don't go getting all depressed on me again," Fiona warned her. "This is my last day off and I don't want to spend it in misery. What say we do a bit of exploring? Are you up to a walk of about half an hour?"

Imogen nodded, "I think so."

"Good. There's a sort of a cliff edge with a pretty good view away to the east of town. If we set off now, we can be there and back before the sun gets too unbearable. Then we can flake out for the rest of the day."

The path wound through the edge of town for a few hundred yards before branching off into the bush. People greeted Fiona with pleasure as they passed each compound and in no time at all they had a following of children. "Sistah-Fionah." The emphasis on the last syllable of each word gave their calls an exotic sound to Imogen's ears. She loved the rhythm and cadence of Ghanaian speech, whether in Twi or English, but she could not make out the rhyme which the children seemed to be repeating over and over. "What are they saying?" She turned to Fiona for clarification.

"Oh, it's just a nonsense rhyme. They shout it whenever they see an 'oberuni', even the translation makes no sense to me. I'm so used to it now I don't hear it, but it used to drive me barmy." She stopped for a moment to talk with an old woman. While she waited, Imogen watched the children, playing a sort of peekaboo with the braver ones. She felt in her pocket, pulling out a coin and soon had a fascinated audience as she 'walked' it through and over her fingers. The children whispered and pushed at each other for a better view, their eyes wide. Seeing Fiona was ready to move on, Imogen finished her performance by causing the coin to disappear from her hand and reappear behind the ear of a boy of about four. The children, as one, gave a delighted gasp.

"Come on, maestro," Fiona laughed. "They'll keep you here all day if you'll do that for them."

As they went further from the town, the children fell away behind them and soon the only sounds came from their own feet and the surrounding bush. There was a blue-green flash across the path in front of them and Fiona pointed into a nearby banana tree. A brilliant sunbird was drinking from the flowers, its metallic blue and green feathers shimmering on its head and back as it twisted and turned in the sunlight. They passed a pair of black and red butterflies circling in an endless dance, up, down, around and over each other. Again the colours were superb. Imogen was suddenly reminded of her wish for a video camera.

It wasn't long before they reached a sudden bend in the path and a view opened out beneath them. Osubuso was near the top of the escarpment which ran at an angle across the lower third of the country, so they hadn't far to climb for this reward. Imogen stared at the scene. The ground fell away quite sharply, with some exposed and dramatic looking bluffs not far from where they stood. Below them, the flatter land stretched off into the distance, eventually merging with the sky in a red-brown haze. A few plumes of smoke gave away the location of the villages scattered across the plain.

"I like to come and sit here every so often," Fiona said. "It can get a bit claustrophobic staying on the compound too long. And it's far enough that I usually don't get followed, so I get a bit of peace too. When the air's clearer, in the rainy season, it feels like you can see the lake over there," she waved her arm south and east, the direction in which Lake Volta lay, "but it's probably an illusion. We're not that close really."

"It's a grand view." Imogen agreed. "That was one thing I found strange about Dhaka, it was so flat. I shouldn't have been surprised, I mean I knew it was flat, but it made me realise how much I look for landmarks in the country around me. I couldn't get my bearings at all."

"Tell me more about what it was like. From what you said before it seems you thought the Bangladeshis more enterprising than the Ghanaians."

"I did think that at first, but I'm not sure now, after the people I've seen here. I think it's more just the contrast between an urban population and a rural one. The pace of life is so different. Here it's more steady so it's easy to think nothing is happening. Dhaka was all hustle and bustle."

"I'm not sure how I'd take to that. I like my space."

Imogen was thoughtful. "I know what you mean, but the people there seemed to have an amazing capacity to make their own space, right in the middle of the street. I mean, you'd see them washing right in the middle of everybody, and yet it was as if they were in a private bathroom. I suppose it's necessity really."

"I've noticed here, in Accra at least, it's sort of as if people don't actually look at those private moments, whereas we stare, because they are so private." Fiona said.

"Yes, I think so. It's another of those contrasts. The bustle of a busy street and the stillness and inward focus of a bathing man or woman. Like the wealth and the beggars, and the squalor and the brightness of the clothes. The other thing missing here is the cycle-rickshaw." Imogen thought for a moment. "There's no equivalent. The rickshaw riders are incredible, death-defying. I'd be terrified but they weave in and out of the rest of the traffic with just a hair's breadth to spare every time. The loads they manage to balance on them are enormous. I even saw one actually transporting a man and his motorbike. Then you see the riders fast asleep lying across the saddle and handlebars as if they were as wide as a double bed."

"I suppose people can adapt to anything if they have to." Fiona glanced at her watch. "We better get back before it gets too hot, I don't want to tire you out." She looked up at the sky. "Those clouds seem to be coming closer, it's almost like I can smell them. Maybe it really will rain today. I hoped it would a couple of days ago but nothing came of it."

They made their way back down the gentle slope towards the town. Imogen spoke after a long silence. "You know what you were saying about good imagery being needed for fundraising?"

"Yes."

"Well, can I try an idea out on you?"

"Go ahead."

"When we arrived last week to all that singing and dancing I wished I'd brought a video camera with me to capture the scene and it set me thinking. How about proposing to Nigel that we make a video of the project here as a publicity venture, showing all the different activities you provide?" Her voice was eager.

"Have you done much video work?" Fiona asked, thinking of the hours of amateur video she had been forced to watch over the years.

"No, but it can't be that hard," Imogen sensed her reluctance. "But if you won't even consider it." Her face settled into a scowl.

Fiona, looking up, laughed. "Now, now, don't get into a sulk. That's not what I said at all. I'm just not sure why you want to branch out into video when you're already more than able to do the job with an ordinary camera or a sketch pad. An amateur video isn't going to impress Nigel as an idea, is it?"

"I s'pose not, but do you think it's a reasonable idea?" Imogen was still unhappy.

"It's got potential. It would depend very much on how you went about it." Fiona relented, adding, "Tell me more about what you'd like to do."

Imogen spoke slowly. "Well, I thought about showing the different things you all do in the project; the clinic, the co-ops, farming, you know, everything. To give people back in the UK an idea of where the money goes and how important it is."

"I don't see why you shouldn't give it a try, but what about expanding it beyond the project? Showing people at home a little bit of real life here so that they understand people don't just sit about waiting for their money to arrive."

"Well, I don't know. I thought the only way to make the connection was through the money angle, you know, a sort of personal link. I was thinking of it as PR for ActionFirst, so it would have to be about the project, wouldn't it?"

"I can see that," Fiona agreed, "but you can't pretend that it's so one-sided. I wouldn't be happy with such a distortion of our work at all."

"But it has to show the project off to advantage, otherwise there's no point." Imogen walked a few steps in silence as she thought. "It would show the difference the project was making to the daily lives of people here, wouldn't that be enough?"

"It needs to show how much they do for themselves, that really the project couldn't succeed without them. Not the other way around." Fiona's expression, unusually for her, gave a clear indication of the strength of her feelings on the issue.

"OK, so I could maybe focus on a few of the people here, and then show how the project has helped them succeed?" Fiona nodded, confirming that was a more appropriate balance. "So, you'd be happy for me to go ahead and ask Nigel, then?"

"Yes, but wait till you're well away from here. It's probably better if he doesn't think we've spoken about it. He likes to have his own publicity ideas, really, but go on, give it a bash. The worst he can do is say 'no'."

"OK, I will." Imogen was surprised to find they were nearly at the house. The conversation had taken her attention completely. Not even the children's enthusiastic greetings had got through. Still distracted she went to find her notebook and spent the next few hours trying to organise her ideas more coherently. Nigel would take some persuading, but she could be tenacious when she really wanted something.

12

Fiona stood on the verandah feeling the wind blow cool on her face. Now she really could smell the rain coming: an intoxicating mix of rich earthy odours and cool moist air. At last! She went back inside to find Imogen. She wanted to share her excitement with somebody. She tapped at Imogen's door and went in. "It's going to rain, it's really going to rain. Isn't that wonderful!"

Imogen looked up, responding immediately to the eagerness in Fiona's manner. "Really? I noticed it was a bit dark, but I just thought it must be getting late."

"Come out and watch it with me?"

They went back to the verandah and sat in the rather rickety chairs watching the onrushing storm. The sky was completely filled with purple-black clouds, and the wind was strengthening rapidly. "Don't you just love it, that wind on your face?" A huge bolt of lightning split the sky in front of them, followed almost instantaneously by a crunching thunderclap. Fiona clasped her hands together in glee. "I love thunderstorms, don't you?"

This one was more dramatic than any Imogen had known, but Fiona's enthusiasm was infectious. Beyond the hedge she saw people scurrying for cover. "What are they all running for, I thought they'd be out singing and dancing in it after waiting so long."

"Not the Ghanaians." Fiona laughed, "They don't like the rain, nor the sun, in fact they're not too keen on any sort of weather. I've only seen them voluntarily out in the elements once, and then it was only the little kids. It was a hailstorm. It was hilarious. They were trying to collect the hailstones and couldn't understand why their prizes kept disappearing before they could carry them off to show everyone."

The wind grew stronger still, tossing the trees wildly. A few large drops of rain fell, causing the dust to flare up and swirl in the gale. In just a few seconds the rain grew to a steady downpour, then a torrent, and the wind eased. Imogen was amazed at how quickly the parched ground became a mass of rivulets. Rain thrummed on the corrugated iron roof and, flowing fiercely, sluiced over the guttering. There was another flash and rumble, but this time not quite so close.

Suddenly Fiona leapt up and ran out into the garden. She was instantly soaked to the skin. She raised her arms and spun crazily around. "Oh, water, water, wonderful water! Come on Imogen, come out in it. It's too good to miss."

"Are you crazy?" Imogen stayed in the shelter of the verandah watching her hostess cavorting about. Her drenched clothes clung to her body and Imogen couldn't help but appreciate the curves that this revealed.

"Yes, I am. Come on, don't be a spoilsport. I've waited nearly six months for this." Fiona begged, coming up to the porch and catching Imogen's hand. "Please?" So Imogen gave in, shuddering with surprise at the coldness of the rain on her body, but soon swooping and running as madly as Fiona.

The lunacy wore off after a few minutes and they retreated onto the porch again. Standing in two rapidly expanding puddles, they regarded each other solemnly for a moment. Then the giggles began and soon they were helpless with laughter. "Just look at us," Fiona wheezed. "Two grown women playing in the rain like idiots. Do you think anyone saw us?"

"You said they'd all be inside. I hope so, or they'll be wondering whether they should visit the clinic anymore," Imogen spluttered with mirth. "Who wants a loony for a midwife?"

"Oh, I know, it was mad, but I just had to." Slowly Fiona sobered up. The sight of Imogen's sodden clothing brought a pang of guilt, and another emotion she was unwilling to specify. "We better get out of these wet things, especially you. I shouldn't have made you do it, not after you've been sick." She turned to go inside, but Imogen caught her hand. "I'm glad you did, I haven't had such a good laugh in ages. Thanks." She bent forward and kissed Fiona, her own lips deliciously cool with rainwater.

There was a moment of stillness then Fiona broke away and the moment passed. "Come on, I'll get us some towels." They each went into a bedroom to emerge a while later dry, respectable, mature adults.

But when it came time to say goodbye after lunch the next day, their embrace was a little closer and lasted just a little longer.

Part Two: *Signs of Growth*.

13

"These are excellent, Imogen my dear, really excellent." Nigel spread the photos out on the table before him, examining them closely. He picked up one showing a man and woman working together on a farm. They were a dusty grey colour from the ash which blew up around their feet. The woman had paused to wipe her face and the two were obviously sharing a joke, their faces joyful under the patina of sweat and dust. Behind the man, the freshly turned ground bore testament to their joint labours. Nigel looked up at Imogen. "You have a real eye for this work. I'm delighted with what you've produced and bang on schedule too." Nigel nodded again his mind already running through ideas for using the photos to ActionFirst's advantage.

Imogen spoke quietly. "I'm glad you feel I've done a good job. The whole project was an important learning experience for me, too."

"Mmmm, good." Nigel's own thoughts were distracting him as usual. "Damn. I wish we had the funds to employ you permanently, my dear, but I know the Board would never swallow that. I hate to think of you working for another agency. I like to feel we have a certain edge when it comes to our publicity and fundraising work." He tapped his fingers meditatively on the table. "I don't suppose it's fair to ask you to limit your options either, not when you're working freelance," he smiled.

Imogen was amazed how different Nigel was here in his Birmingham office. Apart from the sprinkling of 'my dears' in his speech, the man who had so irritated her in Ghana was almost gone. He was direct, incisive and had none of the pomposity she'd come to associate with him. And there was absolutely no denying his eye for the telling image. She took a deep breath.

"Well, no, I can't do that, but there is something I'd like to discuss with you." Her tone was cautious.

Nigel looked up, his face alert. "Yes."

Remembering Fiona's comment about him liking to feel PR was his domain, Imogen went on carefully. "It's an idea that's been growing over the last few weeks, really. I don't know if you remember the discussion the night before we left Accra?"

Nigel shook his head, "Not particularly, no. Go on."

"Well, we were sort of reviewing the whole visit and something you said set me thinking. You said it was a shame the only time people focused on developing countries was when they were in a crisis and it would be good if there was some way of getting them interested in the ordinary everyday nature of the struggle to survive. Crisis was just the tip of the iceberg, I think that was the phrase you used."

Imogen stopped as Nigel gave a slight snort, regarding her with amused suspicion. "I don't remember saying any such thing, but carry on. I am intrigued."

"Well, it might not have been those exact words," she admitted, warming to him still further, "but that was the gist of it. I would be very interested to work on developing the idea. I've been thinking of a sort of 'coffee table' book, mainly pictures with some text, to show just that everyday life. You know, like a calendar only more substantial." She stopped and waited.

Nigel returned to his contemplation of her work, still covering the table. "It could work, if we got the balance right. It would need something to give it focus, to create some connection for people who've never been outside the UK." He thought hard, his gaze coming back to her. "Did you have anything in mind for that, an angle to follow?"

"I wondered about the Osubuso project. It has a lot of different aspects to pick up on and touches upon several areas of ordinary life, and different population groups." Imogen felt a knot of tension in her stomach, unable to bear the thought that Nigel might suggest somewhere else.

"Yes, it's a good example of what ActionFirst can foster too, shows us in a good light." Nigel appeared to reach an internal decision. "And Fiona Tisdale is just the sort of woman people in the street can identify with; sensible, down to earth and very capable but with something of a mission, too. She'd provide an excellent focal point to keep their interest. Yes, I think Osubuso would do nicely as an example of what ActionFirst's money can achieve. And you have the talent to make it attractive enough as an art book, too, so I think it could be a reasonable venture, with a chance of producing a financial return for us." He moved round the table and stretched out his hand to Imogen. "If you can put a proposal together, budget, outline, production dates, the usual stuff, then I think I could get the Board to back the idea."

"Really?" Imogen let out a long breath and the tension left her body. She broke into a delighted smile as she shook Nigel's hand vigorously. "That's great. I'll get something to you by the end of next week, if that's OK?"

Nigel agreed as he shepherded her out of his office back into the bright June sunshine. It was only as she left the building that Imogen registered what he had said about keeping the focus on the project, and on Fiona in particular. '*Shit. How the hell am I going to talk her into accepting Nigel's version? It's exactly what she said she wouldn't do.*' She shrugged her shoulders, too pleased with the prospect of spending more time in Osubuso to let any negative thoughts intrude. '*Oh, I'll cross that bridge when I come to it, somehow. I'll keep quiet for now, or she'll probably wreck the whole thing by refusing to take part.*'

14

Fiona was restless, not enjoying her Saturday off. The project activities had settled into a new pattern with the arrival of the rain. Kofi Paul was very busy with the agricultural work: everything was growing madly as if in a rush to make up for lost time. The malnourished children had long since left the ward and the clinic work had reverted to a more usual pattern; chest infections, diarrhoea and malaria with the occasional more exotic case or dramatic accident. The maternity unit was as busy as ever and Kofi had begun a new round of out of school and youth clubs in some of the further away villages. Just the day before,

ActionFirst's letter had arrived confirming both three year's funding and that Kofi Paul would become manager once she left. Everything was going well and yet she felt strangely dissatisfied and out of place. True the water and electricity supplies were as erratic as ever but with the rain regularly filling the house tank at least she only had to carry the water from there to the bathroom.

She paced round the house as she tried to put her finger on the cause of her trouble. '*Probably just cabin fever,*' she told herself, '*you haven't been out of Osubuso for almost three months.*' Comfort Atta was away on her annual leave, so there was little chance of getting time off. '*That means at least another six weeks before I can get away,*' Fiona sighed heavily. She hadn't felt this way since her first few months in Osubuso.

And it wasn't just cabin fever, although she was trying hard to convince herself. The letter, so full of good news, such a cause for celebration, had a sting in the tail. Nigel had written that Imogen would be coming to work on her picture book idea, and it was his description of this that had really upset Fiona. He'd called it 'a book to show the essential nature of the work you and the project have done with ActionFirst money'. Nothing there about any contribution the local people made, and worse still, implying that she was the central force behind everything that did happen. She couldn't believe Imogen had really caved in so totally, even given that the whole idea depended on Nigel's agreeing to stump up the finance.

For a while, she tried to distract herself with music, letter writing and books, but without much success. Finally she decided on baking bread as at least she could take out her frustrations on the dough. She was just beginning the second round of vigorous kneading when she heard a car pull up outside the house. She replaced the damp tea-towel over the dough and wiped her hands, it would keep for a few more minutes while she dealt with whoever had arrived.

Before she reached the door two small bodies came hurtling through it towards her. "Auntie Fi, Auntie Fi, we're here. We came to see you." It was Terry and Jack, with their parents Rebecca and David close behind. "It's a prize," three year old Jack piped up, grabbing her hand.

"You mean a surprise," said Terry instructively, a little more reserved at almost six years of age.

"Well, whatever it is, it's lovely." Fiona scooped them both into her arms hugging them tightly. "What on earth are you doing here?" The question was directed at Rebecca and David along with another round of welcoming embraces.

"I had to go and check up on a problem at one of the producers near Kumasi and Rebecca felt like getting out of Accra, and we all thought we should check up on you as we haven't seen you in ages." David grinned at her as he shook his shaggy crop of blond hair out of his eyes. He worked for a company which raised, slaughtered, packaged and marketed chickens. Fiona loved the sign outside the main outlet in Accra. It bore a picture of a plump white chicken, in a bow-tie and dark glasses, carrying a briefcase under one wing, with the words 'Fat, dressed and ready to go' emblazoned in bold black capitals underneath.

"So how are you?" Rebecca asked taking her arm. "How did the visit go?"

Before Fiona could reply Jack reclaimed her attention. "Auntie Fi, why have you got white stuff all over your head?"

"Oh dear, have I?" she laughed. "I've been making bread, Jack, and I must have got the flour in my hair. Does it look very bad?"

"You look like Granny," said Jack. "How do you make bread?"

"It's quite hard work and needs somebody strong. Would you like to help me finish it off?" Both boys jumped at the chance, demonstrating real enthusiasm if not effectiveness. The next half an hour passed quickly. Rebecca made a pot of tea and she and David sat waiting for the chance of adult conversation once the boys' excitement abated.

Leaving the bread to rise again, Fiona led the boys out of the kitchen. "I'm just going to pop them over to Felicia's, I'll be back in a tick." She mouthed the word 'puppies' in answer to Rebecca's inquiring look.

"That should keep them away for a while," Fiona said as she flopped down into a chair a few moments later. "Now, where were we? Oh, it's so good to see you both. I meant to get down ages ago but the ActionFirst evaluation visit got extended slightly, and then Comfort Atta went on leave."

"We were half expecting you," said David. "That's partly why we made this a family outing. Rebecca was worried you'd be going crazy up here."

"Was it awful, then?" Rebecca asked, concerned. Fiona was not looking her usual cheerful self. "They can't have given you a bad report, surely?"

"No, no, just the opposite in fact." Fiona brightened as she told them of the project's secure funding and the decision about Kofi Paul.

"Brilliant, so why did they end up staying so long then?"

"Only one of them did, the photographer, a woman called Imogen, who Nigel hadn't even told me was coming." Fiona replied. "She had to stay here, as the Presby only has the two rooms, and then she went down with malaria the night before they were due to go to Bolga. That was the weekend I would have come down to see you, but..." she raised her hands.

"You poor thing," Rebecca was sympathetic. "What a nightmare. How come she got malaria?"

"She wasn't taking any prophylaxis," Fiona explained.

"Well, that's just plain thoughtless." David exclaimed. "Putting you to all the trouble of looking after her just because she was too stupid to protect herself. I hope you told her what for."

"I didn't see the point in adding to her misery."

"No, you wouldn't would you?" This time it was Rebecca who was indignant. "You're far too soft on people, Fiona. You need to look after yourself a bit more. You're looking really tired and it's not as if this job's a rest cure either." Rebecca's scolding was half-hearted, she knew her words would make little difference. She and David had got to know Fiona not long after her arrival in Ghana. She'd been in Accra for a few weeks orientation. Rebecca had been part of the team responsible for language training. They'd taken to each other immediately, a friendship cemented when Fiona helped Rebecca cope with both boys having measles at once.

"It was quite nice to have the company, really. I didn't mind. Imogen's an interesting woman. She's a sculptor but does photography and sketching too. I saw some of her drawings and they were really special. We got on well, so it wasn't difficult."

"Are you keeping in touch with her, then?" David was always wishing Fiona into any potential relationship. He raised an eyebrow, "Will she come back and visit again?"

Fiona smiled indulgently at him. "Well, she will actually, in September, but it's to do with work, not me. She had some idea about making a photographic book about the project. She seems to have persuaded Nigel to back it." Fiona changed the subject, before her unresolved emotions on that topic spilled out. "But what about you two? You're looking particularly glowing, Rebecca."

A slightly shy look came over Rebecca. There was a definite bloom to her dark features and Fiona's midwifery brain suddenly clicked into action. "You're pregnant, aren't you? How wonderful! Congratulations!" She jumped up and hugged them both again.

"It's due in November," Rebecca confirmed. "And I'm feeling really well this time, haven't had any morning sickness at all." She beamed at Fiona as David took her hand and raised it to his lips. "She does look beautiful, doesn't she?" he said lovingly. "We're hoping for a girl this time," he added, eyes shining.

They were still deep in baby talk when the boys returned full of excitement about the puppies they'd seen at Felicia's. "Does it mean we'll get five brothers and sisters when you have your babies, Mummy? Where will we put them all?" Jack's face was solemn.

Rebecca reassured him that there would only be the one, careful to keep her amusement out of her voice. All too soon the time came for them to leave and with more hugs and kisses all round they piled into the car and were gone, leaving the house feeling even emptier than it had before their arrival.

Fiona took the loaves out of the oven, noticing that with the boys' intervention they had not risen quite so well as usual. She began to methodically clean and tidy the kitchen, restoring it to order after the impact of entertaining such active visitors. She looked out from the kitchen over her modest patch of garden, now a mass of green growth and colour. Everything, it seemed, was bursting with life, but she felt her earlier gloom returning. Normally content in her own company, Fiona was able to pass long periods of time in the comparative isolation of Osubuso without any sense of loneliness. But the easy physicality of the two small children, and David and Rebecca's pleasure in each other's company, had left her with an aching longing.

She found herself thinking about Miranda. Their relationship of several years had ended not long before her decision to come to Osubuso. She'd still missed Miranda dreadfully in those early weeks, constantly reliving the way the relationship had gone so wrong. '*I know I get wrapped up in my work,*' Fiona thought, more sad than angry now at the memory, '*but I made up for it when I was off-duty, didn't I?*' She shook her head, remembering Miranda's words. "It's not enough just to have your attention for one week in ten, you know. Yes, I know you love your work, but what about me?" And, although Fiona had countered with the statement that she gave Miranda one hundred and ten percent attention whenever her work allowed, this too had gone against her. She was told it was unreasonable to expect her lover to suddenly drop everything just because she was ready for some fun. In the end Miranda had found Fiona's long periods of mental and emotional distraction too difficult to manage and decided an on-off relationship wasn't for her.

"At least I don't have to struggle with that anymore," she muttered to herself. "Here I can be as much of a workaholic as I like." Moving outside to weed the vegetable patch she pushed away the voice in her head that said "oh yeah?" and the memory of a rain soaked kiss.

Part Three: *An Abundance of Life.*

15

Fiona stood in the crowd outside the airport building scanning the emerging passengers. There she was. The jolt of pleasure as she recognised Imogen surprised her in its intensity. She pushed her way through the people around her and raised her arm, waving, as Imogen came through the doorway. "Imogen. Over here." The relief on Imogen's face was plain as Fiona finally emerged out of the anonymous crowds in front of her.

"Oh, there you are. I don't remember it being so busy when I came with the others," she laughed hugging Fiona to her for a moment. "It's good to see you."

"Akwaaba." Fiona smiled back at her warmly. "Here, let me help with your bags. My god, what have you brought, a whole photographic studio?" She surveyed the pile of luggage on the trolley, guarded jealously by one of the many porters. It was a sharp reminder of her anger over the direction the book project seemed to be going, but she was determined not to let her feelings show. "On second thoughts we'll just let him struggle with it, shall we?" She gave the porter instructions, pointing in the direction of the vehicle. Then she shepherded Imogen through the crowd towards the relative calm of the car park. "So, did you have a good journey? It's a bit of an early start when you have to get that connection in Amsterdam. Did you catch up with your beauty sleep on the plane?"

"No, not really. I was too busy staring out at the Sahara. It's magnificent, isn't it? Last time it was too hazy to see anything clearly, but this time, I mean, I could see every detail. Incredible." Imogen waved her hands and shook her head with amazement, causing Fiona to chuckle to herself. She had forgotten just how vivacious her visitor could be.

"Here we are," Fiona unlocked the doors and pointed the

porter towards the back of the large Nissan all-terrain vehicle.

"Careful with that one." said Imogen, stretching forward to prevent one of the metal cases tumbling onto the floor. "Let me pack them in properly. The stuff is well cushioned inside but it's best if they don't actually fall on top of each other during the journey." She shifted the cases around until she had them wedged firmly between the two back seats. "That should do it, even on your roads."

Fiona paid the porter giving him a little extra as she normally did. "All set?" she inquired. "OK then, let's get off. I'm sorry to whisk you away like this but I do have to be back at Osubuso as soon as possible." She manoeuvred the heavy vehicle through the traffic and out onto the highway. "Ideally, you should be getting a good night's rest here in Accra before coming up to the project."

"Don't worry about it," Imogen replied happily. "I really don't feel that tired, I'm too excited." She flashed a grin at her companion. "It's very good of you to meet me at all. Is the clinic very busy, then?"

"It's not any busier than usual, it's just that Agnes isn't back from her leave for another few days, so there's only been two of us to share the on-call. It makes it more difficult to get any real time away." Fiona was silent for a time, concentrating on negotiating her way through the lanes of traffic and several busy junctions. Imogen was content to stare out of the window allowing her mind to assimilate the changing nighttime scenery. She remembered the taxis with their characteristic yellow paint on each front and back wing, and the noise of car horns, mixing with shouting voices as they passed a small bus station. She shut her eyes for a moment, allowing the smells to bombard her through the open car window: an exotic mix of dust, smoke, compost and car exhausts, overlaid with the sweetness of spices and cooking oil from the chop-bars which lined both sides of the road. Suddenly she felt she'd only been away a couple of weeks, not several months.

It took about forty minutes to get clear of the city but once they were on the open road, Fiona relaxed. "Sorry," she said. "I don't much like driving in Accra." She glanced over at Imogen. "You've had your hair cut. It looks nice, it suits you shorter."

"Thanks. I thought it would be better. I remember how it felt hot and sticky all round my neck before. It's cool this way." Imogen ran her fingers over her head raising little spikes of hair. "I don't know how you manage with long hair."

Fiona pulled a face. "I had to let it grow when I couldn't find anyone to cut it properly, but I've got used to it now. I keep it tied up nearly all the time."

Imogen held her hand out of the window creating a pleasant breeze on her face as the car sped through the darkness. Now they were out of the city the air was cooler filling her senses with new combinations of sound and fragrance. "The air smells fresher than I remember. I suppose that's because it's not harmattan season now?"

"Yes, it is. It's a pity you can't see much in the dark. You'd really notice a difference. Everything's grown again, but never mind, you'll see in the morning at Osubuso how green and lush everywhere is. The staff are really excited about your visit, and the book and everything, you know." Fiona changed gear as they overtook a lorry carrying three huge tree trunks.

Imogen twisted in her seat to look back out of the window. "Did you see that? It was all skewiff. The back wheels aren't in line with the front ones at all." She turned an incredulous face back to Fiona, who smiled. "It's best not to think about the state of the other vehicles on the road," she said. "It's often the tree trunks that are holding the whole thing together with the timber lorries, but at least that one had lights." Her features turned serious again at Imogen's growing horror. "Quite often the truck drivers only put on their lights when they see another vehicle coming. As you can imagine there are some horrific accidents. Usually I try not to do any night driving, only if there's an emergency to the hospital, or a special reason, like tonight."

"Don't tell me anymore," Imogen shuddered. "I don't want to know. I'll have nightmares all week." But she was successfully distracted when Fiona asked her about an exhibition of avant garde photography she'd mentioned in one of her letters.

The miles passed quickly. Fiona drew the car to a halt outside her house in Osubuso. She looked at her watch, noting it was well after midnight. "Let's get this stuff inside and then you can get off to bed." She turned back to Imogen, a sudden thought striking her. "I hope you're not allergic to cats? I was given a couple of kittens last week by a woman in one of the co-op groups."

Imogen, carrying three of the cases into the house, shook her head. "No, I love cats, they won't worry me at all." She put down the cases and returned to the car to help Fiona with the remaining items. "I could murder a cup of tea before I turn in. Is it OK if I make one?"

"Go right ahead," replied Fiona, "and don't stand on ceremony while you're here. Just treat the place as if it was yours and help yourself to whatever you need. OK?" Imogen nodded and went into the kitchen where she located all the necessary items easily. Returning with a cup of tea in each hand she found Fiona sitting with both kittens on her lap.

"Meet Nkatia and Kelewele. Aren't they lovely?" She held up the two furry bundles, one in each hand. Both kittens were grey in colour, one completely covered with tiger stripes and the other a dark, mottled pattern but with pure white patches under its chin, covering three of its feet and the tip of its tail. They were just eight weeks old.

Imogen put down the tea and took a closer look at the kittens. "They're gorgeous. What d'you say their names are?"

"This one's Nkatia," Fiona pointed to the striped kitten, "and this one's Kelewele. They are such greedy little things I just had to call them after food. 'Nkatia' means groundnuts and 'Kelewele' is small slices of fried ripe plantain." She scratched behind Kelewele's ears and the kitten purred contentedly. "They're good company but full of mischief, so watch out," she warned Imogen. Nkatia jumped down off Fiona's lap and came over to investigate the new arrival in the house, climbing onto Imogen's chair with ease. The kitten settled in the crook of Imogen's elbow and looked steadily up into her face. She reached a finger to tickle under its chin. "Well? Do I pass inspection then?" Nkatia's eyes closed and she too began to purr. Fiona and Imogen looked at each other and burst out laughing. Startled, both kittens leapt down and disappeared.

Finishing her tea, Imogen yawned. "I'm off to bed then, see you in the morning."

"Yes. You're sure you've got everything you need? OK. Sound

sleep." Fiona, too, headed for bed, very pleased that so far she had managed not to reveal anything of her annoyance about the book.

<u>16</u>

In the morning all the staff gathered to greet Imogen and, as before, they expressed their welcome in song. Their delight increased still further when Imogen brought out the small gifts she had purchased. Fiona had suggested she bring small souvenirs with some connection to Manchester. Imogen had added an individual photographic portrait for each staff member complete with a simple frame. There was a general hubbub as they all examined each others' pictures.

"What an inspiration, Imogen. I'd never have thought of anything so personal, and to actually have taken all the individual photos while you were here, it's brilliant. They'll be falling over themselves to help you now," Fiona said, smiling.

"I had a moment of panic, thinking maybe I hadn't got one of everybody, but I was able to enlarge some of the group shots and get the ones that were missing that way." Imogen replied. "I've got some for you, too, but I'll get them out later, if you don't mind. I want you to have time to look at them properly."

Most of the staff were eventually persuaded to go and get on with their work, leaving Kofi Paul, Kofi and Comfort Atta to discuss plans with Imogen and Fiona. Fiona could feel tension spread across her shoulders, there would be no avoiding the argument now. She was still determined to remain calm, but as she listened to Imogen's description of the book's likely content, it became a losing battle.

"So what I need to do is capture all the different activities in the project," Imogen was saying, "and emphasise the ways in which you help the local people towards a better life. Mr Fulford was very clear that this book needs to show people in the UK where their money goes, the things that can only happen because they have given that money."

The three Ghanaians were listening attentively. Fiona knew that good manners would prevent them from direct disagreement, especially given the way Imogen was emphasising Nigel's particular interest in the project. She shifted in her chair, but still did not speak herself.

"Now, the other thing that Mr Fulford was very clear about was that there had to be something in the book that would make a connection for people in the UK. His feeling was that the most straightforward way to do this was by making Fiona's role here a central part of what the book is about. That doesn't mean I don't focus on all the rest of you, of course," Imogen rushed on, now sure that her intuition that this would upset Fiona had been spot on. "It's just that to a UK audience obviously Fiona will be a more familiar figure than anyone else here in Osubuso."

"No, no and no." Fiona's anger finally boiled over. "That's the last straw. I was willing to go along with it all being focused on the project instead of people's struggle to survive, but this I can't accept. Making it look as if I'm the central force when we all know that's a completely false picture."

Imogen's face fell. She swallowed audibly, then opened her mouth but no words came. There was a moment of deathly silence, broken, of course, by Kofi Paul. "But Fiona, don't get so upset. After all, you are the manager, and you have had an important impact on the way we have all developed. We will all be in the book, but I think Nigel is right to see you as a central figure."

The other two nodded, and Imogen gave Kofi Paul a grateful glance.

But his diplomacy was not to be successful this time. Fiona was adamant. "No, Kofi Paul, I can't let it happen that way. I couldn't have achieved one single thing without the rest of you being here to support and guide me. I won't be a part of anything that implies it was the other way around." Fiona stood up, knowing she should leave before making it impossible for Imogen to proceed at all. "I'm sorry, but I just can't do it. I realise that the book still has to be made, but I don't want any further part of it. The four of you will have to sort something out without me. I'm going to see to the clinic before ...." She bit off the last words abruptly with a piercing look in Imogen's direction and stalked out of the house.

Imogen stared glumly at the table top as the silence lengthened. But she had to salvage something. "I'm sorry if these ideas don't seem right to you," she said, "and I understand why Fiona feels so strongly. She's right that all of you are important, but Nigel knows what ActionFirst needs, too, and they're paying for it all." She looked round at each of her companions in turn. "I confess, I'm not sure where we go from here."

Comfort Atta spoke for the first time. "Both of them, Sister Fiona and Mr Fulford, are right, and what we have to do is find a way to do what both of them want. I'm sure we can work it out if we all put our minds together, then everyone can be happy with your book." She smiled reassuringly at Imogen. "Don't you think so Kofi, Kofi Paul?"

"Yes, of course, it's a matter of balance. May I?" Kofi reached over and took a piece of paper from Imogen's notepad, and a pencil. "I always need to write things down in order to think clearly. So, what objectives do we have for this book? Let's start with Nigel's and those of ActionFirst, then we'll add everyone else's, and then we'll work out a way of achieving it." He began to draw up a list as the others offered their suggestions, and eventually a consensus emerged. Imogen would follow each of the senior staff, Fiona included, building up a picture of their role in the project, but interweaving this with images to show how their work only built upon the efforts made by local people to improve their circumstances. By the end of a couple of hours, they were all feeling enthusiastic, and very pleased with themselves.

Imogen thanked them warmly, both excited and a little awed by what she now had to achieve. "If I can create a book which gives people in the UK even just a notion of how inventive and resourceful you people in Osubuso are, I'll be really pleased. And I think I can manage it, knowing I've got the three of you along side. Thank you all for your time, and for coming up with such an ingenious compromise. I know Fiona will like it now, and I'm sure Nigel will see how the end result is even better than his original plan."

Fiona came in for the midday meal, but was silent.

Imogen rose from her seat and went into her room, returning

with a carrier bag and a flat package. She placed them beside Fiona on the table. "It's just a small contribution to the household supplies, and some photos I chose for you," she said quietly, sitting down again.

"Marmite, cheese, olives, pickle," Fiona enumerated each item as she spread them out in front of her. "Jelly, oatmeal biscuits, tinned pudding." She looked up, trying to recover her manners. "Oh, and Thornton's toffee. You really shouldn't have, Imogen, it's too much."

"I just tried to think of what would be difficult to get here, and what you might be missing from home." Imogen pushed the flat package towards her. "These are your photos."

Inside the paper Fiona found half a dozen pictures of herself bathing a baby. They were taken without flash and so kept the softness of the dimly lit nighttime labour ward.

"Do you like them?"

Fiona lifted her eyes from the pictures. "You've caught it perfectly, the pleasure of bathing a newborn baby. You even managed to make me look human in the middle of the night, too." A shyness came into her face as she went on, "I usually hate photos of me, but there's something different about these."

"You were so focused on what you were doing I don't think you were aware of anything else at all, that's what I was trying to capture, the communion between you and the baby."

Fiona put the photos to one side, clearing her throat. "About this morning. I'm sorry I went off like that, but I've been brooding on the whole business on and off for months. It isn't fair to blame you when I know you have to carry out the work the way Nigel wants." She looked up at Imogen. "I'll just have to swallow my principles so that you can do what you're being paid to do," she offered with a wry smile.

"Hopefully you won't have to." Imogen replied. "Maybe I should have been more forceful with Nigel, but I was just so pleased to have the chance, I didn't want to risk anything by arguing with him."

"And that's exactly why I shouldn't have got angry with you, and especially not in front of everyone like that. In the past I've always agreed with Nigel's views on publicity, but this time I really do think he's wrong."

"Turns out you're not alone," Imogen said with a smile. "There's been a mutiny. Your colleagues and I have spent the morning working out a way to do what we think is best and bugger Nigel. No, that's not true," she added quickly, "but those three came up with a solution which should please him and still allow you to feel comfortable as well."

17

Over the next couple of weeks Imogen spent her time following the senior Ghanaian staff like a shadow. They'd agreed that she would deal with each area of activity in turn, beginning with Kofi's educational and small scale economic projects and finishing with the clinical work and Fiona's managerial role. Kofi introduced her to two of the more active women's co-operative groups, each consisting of about half a dozen women.

She had visited one group with a bee-keeping project from which they had established a successful honey and beeswax candle business. She'd been to the market with one of the women and spent a fascinated day watching her deal with her customers. "She could run a whole course on customer relations, really." Imogen said to Fiona. "I mean she's got it all perfect; the patter, the knowledge of each individual customer, the way to persuade them into buying just a little more than they intended. She's incredible. One guy came up to her and she remembered him from weeks before, asked about his kids and his elderly mother. She talked to him for about twenty minutes before she even asked whether he wanted any honey or candles."

"Well, the Ashanti people are renowned for their trading, you know. They used to maintain a commercial network across the whole of west Africa." Fiona responded. "Kumasi's still a really important trading centre. The market's huge, easily as big as a football ground."

Imogen was also present for the harvesting of the honey. Kofi provided her with a large, unwieldy square of mosquito netting to protect herself. As they made their way through the bush to the hives she asked him, a little apprehensively, "Are you sure I'll be alright with just this net? I've heard African bees are the most vicious in the world."

"You'll be fine, so long as you don't come too close." He reassured her, his dark features creasing into a smile. "You have got the zoom lens, haven't you? Fine. You just tell me if someone needs to move out of the way. Don't worry." He explained again how the smoke would sedate and confuse the bees, making it highly unlikely they would sting anyone. "The women have only ever had one sting in the two years they've been working with the bees. They know what they're doing."

It took Imogen a while to sort out the conflicting requirements of protection from the bees and freedom of movement for her camera but she got there in the end through the judicious placement of a strong rubber band around the lens. The two women harvesting the honey worked quietly, each was covered by a net hanging down from a wide brimmed hat, and wore thick gloves. One, Janet, pumped the smoke distributor while the other, with the delightful name of Gifty, lifted the frames containing the honeycomb from the open hives. What with the swirling smoke, the slow zig-zagging of the bees and the way the nets obscured the women's features, the scene was "like something from a Hitchcock film," Imogen murmured to herself, quite forgetting to keep her distance.

Gifty sliced through each honeycomb, letting the harvested portion fall into the waiting buckets and replacing the frame in the hive. There were twelve hives altogether and it took some time to collect the honey. They never harvested more than two thirds, to be sure there was enough left to keep the bees in good condition. By the time they were done, both women were covered in sweat and streaked from the dirty smoke. They brought the full pails over to show Imogen, gladly stripping off their protective gear as they moved away from the immediate vicinity of the bees.

"Now, we have to clean, strain and bottle it," Janet told her. "Then we work the wax into sheets for the candles." Gifty wiped her face with a handkerchief. "It's hot work. Please, have a taste." She held out a small piece of honeycomb.

"It's delicious. Very different to the honey we get back home.

What gives it such a distinctive flavour?" Imogen asked.

"We think it's the flowers from the oil palm plantation down there." Janet waved an arm in the direction of the edge of the escarpment. "The bees seem to go there a lot at certain times of year. The taste is different when the palm is not in flower." They set off back to town and Imogen focused on capturing the work of changing lumps of beeswax into saleable candles.

On the next occasion Kofi took Imogen to a chop-bar in the town run by another co-operative group. The chop-bar's name was derived from a famous tro-tro slogan 'one man no chop'. Tro-tros, large Bedford trucks with open backs, were no longer common but had been ubiquitous throughout west Africa before the advent of smaller Japanese-made vans. These were known less romantically but perhaps more accurately as '18-condemned's, due to their appalling safety record. Each tro-tro had a slogan painted over the cab reflecting the philosophy of the driver or owner. 'One man no chop' summarised the way in which a lone operator found it hard to make ends meet or have any time to himself. The women had chosen 'One woman plenty chop' for the name of their chop-bar, but it was commonly known as 'the One'.

The chop-bar was housed in an open-sided thatched building. Several rough-hewn benches and tables were lined up in the shade of the roof, divided from the kitchen area by a waist high wall of planking. The kitchen was big enough for three cooking stoves, two kerosine and one charcoal, and had shelving for crockery and other utensils. The most substantial part of the building was the store in which these were locked each night, made of solid wooden boards and corrugated iron sheeting.

At the back of the building was an additional shaded space for food preparation. It was here that the fufu pounding was carried out, the chickens were killed and plucked, and any other more messy tasks done. Imogen tried her hand at pounding fufu, intrigued by the simple mechanical look of the women's movements. The regular pounding of the long poles thumping into the sturdy wooden bowls formed a background rhythm to life all over the area. One woman stood and pounded while the another mixed and turned the contents by hand. Imogen's efforts caused much hilarity as she tried unsuccessfully to direct the heavy pole into the bowl, almost upsetting it entirely with one poorly aimed stroke. The women only allowed her one attempt at turning the fufu in the bowl, and that resulted in bruised fingers.

"Never mind, sister," one of them comforted her, "we've been doing this since we were children, and we had plenty of our own bruises before we became skilled."

By midday the chop-bar was busy with a constant stream of predominantly male customers. Fufu, kenkey (balls of fermented maize dough), red-red (a combination of bean stew and kelewele), and yam chips were rapidly consumed along with light soups and stews. The women kept up a continual exchange of repartee with the diners, chiding them for leaving any food, advising them on their love lives and generally bossing them about.

Towards the middle of the afternoon, when the rush seemed over, Imogen asked one of the women, "Where do you get the supplies from?"

"Some of it we grow in our gardens, some of it we buy in the market here in Osubuso, and some we have to go into town for."

"So you buy fresh food each day?"

"Of some things, but not all. We have a freezer where we can store some meat, beef, mutton and goat, not chicken as we get that fresh, so we are able to buy in bulk. That makes it much cheaper." Seeing Imogen was about to ask another question, the woman forestalled her. "We have the freezer through the project loan, when we set up the co-operative group in the beginning. We paid it off last year. You should really talk to Mercy about that. She takes care of the financial side of our group."

"Thank you. I will. Which one is Mercy?" Imogen followed the direction of the woman's hand and moved to talk to Mercy, a large, elderly woman with a belly rumbling laugh.

"Yes, of course you can see the books," Mercy smiled charmingly at Imogen. "Come with me now and I can show you the office." She laughed again. "It's really just a box which I keep the papers in under the bed." The records were meticulously kept in a series of elementary school style notebooks.

"We were all a bit worried about having a loan, at first," Mercy informed her, "but Kofi explained it all and how we would have time to pay it back. And we did in only seven months." There was pride in her voice. "Now we have some savings in the bank, and we can even start another enterprise."

"So what are you going to do next?"

"Well, it won't be another chop-bar, but we have some ideas." Mercy laughed again. "I can't discuss it, I'm afraid. We haven't yet agreed."

Several children came tumbling into the house clamouring for Mercy's attention. School was finished for the day and the kids were in high spirits. They looked neat in their brown and yellow uniforms, thought Imogen, as she succumbed to their entreaties for another display of simple magic tricks.

"Now, now, off with you. Leave my sister in peace. Shoo!" Mercy intervened after a while, allowing Imogen to make her farewells. As she walked back towards the compound she reflected on the warmth and hospitality she encountered everywhere.

<u>18</u>

"No, Nkatia, get down. I'm trying to work." Fiona's voice held an undertone of irritation as she lifted the kitten down from the table for the umpteenth time. She was working on the six-monthly report for ActionFirst and the kitten kept trying to catch the end of her pen as she wrote.

She looked up as Imogen came into the room and put her pen to one side. "How've you got on today then, up at the One?"

"Great." Imogen responded happily. "It all seems to be coming together really well. I've got most of Kofi's stuff on the educational projects and women's co-ops. It's farming next, then the clinical work."

"It's hard to believe you've been here nearly two weeks already. Are you sure you're going to have enough time? When did you say your ticket was booked for?"

"Well, it's booked for October the thirteenth, but it's an open ticket. I can always change it if I need to. How are you getting on with the report?"

"Oh, slowly." Fiona grimaced. "I'd be doing better if it wasn't for that damned cat."

Imogen, who had bent to pick up both Kelewele and Nkatia from where they curled round her ankles, looked up curiously. "Which cat would that be? You can't possibly mean either of these two adorable little angels." She pressed her face into the furry bodies.

"Oh-hoh, can't I just?" said Fiona. "Well, perhaps you can explain to me how to write legibly with a kitten hanging off one end of your pen?" Kelewele had climbed onto Imogen's shoulder and was busy licking behind her ear. The intimacy of the scene made Fiona look away.

Imogen shuddered and removed Kelewele from her perch. "No, Kelewele, you're giving me goosebumps. I can't stand it." She put the kittens on the floor and shooed them away. "I'm sorry, it must be frustrating when you're trying to concentrate. They're very playful, aren't they?" Imogen went through to her room to unload her camera bag.

Fiona snorted, "I'll give them playful." she threatened. Walking into the kitchen she called, "Have you eaten already up at the One or are you ready for some dinner?"

Returning to join her, Imogen replied, "No, I never even thought about eating, but now you mention it, I'm starving. Has Esther left us something delicious again?"

"No. Actually I gave her the afternoon off, she wasn't feeling too good." Fiona opened a cupboard and surveyed the contents, frowning. "What d'you fancy?"

Imogen leaned closer to see what was on offer. "What about pasta? I can make a good sauce with those tomatoes and onions, and I can add a few chopped olives from the ones I brought out. Would that do?"

"Sounds delicious. Are you sure you don't mind cooking?" Fiona's voice was hesitant. "I don't feel it's right, but..."

"You said I was to make myself at home, didn't you? Of course I don't mind." Imogen was firm. "It will be a pleasure."

"OK, that would be lovely. Thanks. I really do need to finish this report." Fiona smiled at her gratefully and went back to the table. It was comforting to hear Imogen moving about in the kitchen as she worked.

"That was scrumptious," she said a couple of hours later, pushing back her empty plate. "How come you cook so well? I had the impression you weren't the domesticated sort."

"No, I'm not really, but I have a thing about pasta and I haven't found anyone who can quite cook it to my satisfaction, so I do it myself." Imogen smiled at her. "It's nice to have someone who appreciates my talent."

"I'm sure you don't want for appreciation, Imogen." Fiona said with a sly look. "Your letters mentioned several women who all seemed desperate to appreciate you."

"Well, yes, I suppose so, but it's not usually my culinary efforts that are the focus of their attention." Imogen replied.

"It must be nice to be so much in demand." Fiona's voice held a tinge of wistfulness, the first indication Imogen had heard that there was anything about her life she would change.

"It is," she concurred, "but it's mostly rather superficial. Once they discover I'm not into artistic angst a lot of women lose interest." She raised an ironic eyebrow. "It would be nice to be wanted for myself rather than as a symbol of someone else's sophistication."

Fiona grew silent, a faraway look in her eyes.

As she cleared away the dishes, Imogen wondered who brought such a wistful expression of longing to Fiona's face. The room was quiet as they each focused on their own work.

"I've done as much as I can bear for tonight. With luck a couple of hours' work tomorrow should see the end of it. Thanks for giving me the space tonight. How about a game of Scrabble?"

"OK."

They were soon absorbed. Imogen watched Fiona's lips move while she concentrated on the letters and board in front of her and wondered about Fiona's past. "That's the best I can do, I think." Fiona turned the board around towards Imogen. "Pickle. That makes you one twenty nine and me one fifty two." Fiona reached for the bag of letters. "And that's the last of the letters." She looked up, catching Imogen's eye. "You better have something good, if you're going to catch me."

"No chance of that," Imogen frowned in mock despair. "Given that you managed to use both the 'q' and the 'z', I don't see how

I'm going to keep myself from a hammering, this time." They were well matched and most games were closely fought, unlike tonight's. "'Evens' is the best I can do." She turned the board back to Fiona.

"You're not as sharp as usual tonight, are you? You could have had 'veneers' across there, see, with the double." Fiona pointed to the left hand corner of the board. "What's distracting you?"

"Oh, I don't know. I'm just not concentrating." Imogen shrugged, tipping the pieces off the board and into the bag as she put away the game.

"Is it something to do with home? You've been quiet since I made that comment about being appreciated. I hope I haven't upset you. I didn't mean to pry, it was just an idle comment." Fiona's concern showed in her voice. "Trust me to put my big foot in it."

"No, you didn't, it's just," Imogen stopped unsure of what exactly was bothering her. She sat back in her chair, lifting her hands behind her head, a contemplative look on her face. "I was just thinking, you know, about relationships and how they never quite turn out how you expect."

"How d'you mean?"

"Well, each time I meet someone new, I think 'yes, this is it', I really do. And then, somehow, within a month or two it all goes wrong, you know?" She glanced over at Fiona, but could not read her expression. "It turns out she's really into heavy metal music, or Japanese paper folding, or worse." Imogen tried to make a joke of it but it didn't quite come off.

Fiona smiled. "You must be mixing with a strange bunch of women if those are examples of their normal pastimes."

"I was speaking metaphorically, as if you didn't know. But there's always something that seems to become an insurmountable barrier after a little while, don't you think?"

Fiona shrugged. "Well, it's no good looking to me for advice. My romantic history is minimal." She laughed but without any real humour.

Imogen raised an eyebrow and waited expectantly for more but nothing materialised. "Oh, no. Don't be such a tease, Fiona, give me a few details at least. I've got quite a bit of history, as you call it, but I wouldn't say my success rate was anything to boast about, either. Just a string of women who all turned out not to be Ms Right."

"Well, there's not much to tell. I was involved with a woman called Miranda. It was very good for quite a while, but you could say she found my work was an insurmountable barrier."

"So how long was a while, and what happened?"

"Oh, about five years altogether, although Miranda would say that only about a fifth of that counted given that the rest of the time she hardly saw me. According to her my priorities were too often elsewhere."

"Where were they then, if you thought she was the one for you?"

"I couldn't find the balance she wanted, I suppose. I tried but there was always some vital thing at work that I couldn't ignore. A woman would take longer than expected in labour or a crisis would occur in one of the families supported by the project. Miranda just got fed up of waiting for me. Looking back I can't blame her really. At least noone else was involved so I didn't have to cope with that sort of rejection." Fiona felt suddenly exposed. "So there you have it, my one-off drama versus your never-ending soap opera. A right pair, aren't we?"

Imogen grinned at her wryly. "Yeah, well, maybe it's a case of the path of true love not running smooth, and all that."

"Or a case of you making your bed but noone finding it fit for lying in," Fiona quipped, happy to have escaped more serious probing.

"Now that's wicked," Imogen laughed, "calling my housekeeping skills into question after I cooked you such a nice tea." She began to giggle as another thought struck her. "Maybe we should swap for a while? I'm sure I could set you up with a few of my cast-offs with an interest in exotic travel. Maybe we could make a business of it." Suddenly, Fiona hiccoughed loudly causing Imogen to laugh all the harder, and she protested at such lack of sympathy. "Oh no, now look what you've done, I hate hiccoughs."

Imogen fetched a glass of water from the kitchen. "Just stand on your head, count backwards from one hundred while holding your nose and drinking this." Fiona took the glass from her as another loud hiccough broke through. She took a deep breath and held it before taking a large mouthful of water. Just as she swallowed it a cushion hit her from behind. "What the hell?" She almost choked, whirling round to find Imogen grinning from ear to ear. "I always find shock therapy works best," she chuckled.

"You pig." Fiona picked up a cushion of her own, swinging it in Imogen's direction.

"But they've gone, haven't they?" Imogen blocked the cushion easily as it came at her head.

"Yes, they have, but even so. I could have choked on my false teeth. Then where would you be?" Fiona sat down, clutching the cushion to her chest and looked accusingly at Imogen.

"Oh, grandmama, I never thought." Imogen, unrepentant, sat opposite her still grinning. "False teeth, my eye. I've seen you tucking into the toffee I brought, you liar. Your teeth are as good as mine." She snapped them together sharply to emphasise her point.

19

"Can I cadge a lift with you this morning? There's something I want to get in Afafranto."

"Yeah, sure, but I can get it for you if you want to get on with stuff here." Fiona said as Imogen walked with her to the car. "What do you need?"

"Well, I was talking with Agnes yesterday and we got round to the state of the ward," Imogen replied. "She told me you haven't decorated in years. I thought I could maybe help out with that, being an artist and all." She grinned at Fiona as she climbed into the front beside her. "I can't get paint in the market here but Agnes said I'd get it in Afafranto."

Fiona looked at her in astonishment. "You're going to paint the ward?"

"At least the labour room anyway. And with a bit of help from my friends." There was a wicked gleam in Imogen's eye.

"Oh yes, and exactly which friends did you have in mind, madam? Remember, I told you already I've no skills in that department." Fiona started the car and they set off on the road down the escarpment. In a while they were speeding along the straight, flat highway into Afafranto, the business and administrative centre of the region. Each intersection they passed was like a mini market with stalls of fruit and vegetables lining the main road for several yards in both directions. In between they passed many other people by the side of the road with goods for sale.

"What are they selling?" Imogen asked. The car was moving too fast for her to make out anything other than the chickens held out by their owners, feet up, heads dangling and wings flapping as if embarrassed by such lack of dignity.

"Snails, freshwater crabs and the odd grasscutter." Fiona replied. "Do you want some?"

"I wouldn't mind a closer look. What's a grasscutter?"

"It's like an enormous rat. It's a favourite bush-meat for Ghanaians. Kofi loves it. We could buy him one if we see a good one." Fiona slowed the car a little looking more carefully at the people they passed. She pulled up at an intersection where several young boys stood, arms extended holding out their wares for inspection. Imogen got out of the car and joined her among them. She left the bargaining to Fiona who she knew enjoyed the banter that went with the haggling. Imogen examined the produce on offer more closely.

The snails and crabs were trussed up like french onions. The crabs were graded in size, largest at the bottom of a string, smallest at the top, tied together with grass. Their pincers waved menacingly in the air. The snail bunches were a work of art in themselves. Each snail had a small hole pierced in the edge of its shell through which grass binding was passed. The grass was then plaited in an elaborate fashion, each string added to the existing bundle to form a thick rope that was finished off in a loop the seller held firmly in his hand. The huge snails, some as much as six inches long, were still alive, climbing stickily over each other with the little freedom their tethers allowed. They looked as tough as boot leather and not at all appetising. Imogen felt her stomach churn.

"This one's a good size and still quite fresh." Fiona claimed her attention and Imogen moved away from the snails. Fiona was holding up a brown furred creature about a foot long and of substantial girth. It was rat-like but had a flatter face, thought Imogen. "It's a grasscutter?" she looked to Fiona for confirmation. "What do they taste like?"

Fiona shook her head. "I have to confess I've never tried one, but Kofi tells me it's delicious."

"I think I'll take his word for it, too, although I suppose I could manage it once it was cooked. But how anyone can eat those snails is beyond me. They look absolutely disgusting." She grimaced as they climbed back into the car and continued their journey. "You haven't tried them, have you?"

"No. I never managed to swallow the French version and these are monstrous." Fiona agreed. "I always imagine chewing them would be like eating rubber."

Imogen found the paint she needed easily in the market in Afafranto. She loved the way the stalls were organised so that each part of the market dealt with a single item. It made shopping a simple business: first the huge piles of mango, pineapple, orange and banana, then carefully measured groups of onion, tomato, carrot and potato. From the mounds of leafy greens in great floppy bunches, Imogen only recognised the kontomire. Further away she made out intriguing piles of spices in a range of earthy colours. Then there were the household goods, fabric and cosmetic stalls, and lots more she had no time to explore. The only areas she shied away from were the fish and meat: the smell and the flies were too much.

On their return to the compound, she changed into some old baggy cut-offs and a T-shirt before taking her selection of paint to show Agnes.

Towards the end of the afternoon, hearing the gales of laughter coming from the building, Fiona wandered over. She stopped in amazement as she came to the labour room doorway. Imogen and Agnes, both somewhat paint-spattered watched as she surveyed their handiwork.

The walls were now a soft pink colour with a dark blue band around the bottom. The ceiling was brilliant white. Even with the old rusty bed the room was transformed. "It's fantastic."

"We've nearly finished. I was just coming to get you." Imogen said. "We need you to help with the final touches." Agnes giggled again beside her, the sound surprising Fiona who had never heard it before. Imogen continued, "I thought we'd put a border round too, about this high." She held her hand about chest high against the wall. "A sort of midwife, mother and baby motif."

"Oh yes? Well, I suppose could lend a hand if you're sure I'll be a help rather than a hindrance." Fiona's puzzlement grew as both women laughed still more. She became suspicious. "Just what are you plotting, Imogen? Come on, tell me."

"Well, actually, your hand is just what we need, and the hands of the mothers and babies in the ward." Imogen drew a breath and spoke more calmly. "I thought we could make hand-prints around the room in a line, mothers, babies and midwives. In the dark blue. What do you think?" Seeing Fiona was still uncertain, Imogen took her hand. "Like this, see?" She dipped the paintbrush into the tin, then drew it across Fiona's hand, turning it to press it firmly against the wall and lifting it off again carefully so as not to smudge the print. Then she took Agnes' hand and repeated the process a few inches along the wall. "We'd put the babies hands in between."

Fiona nodded as the idea became clear. "Yes, definitely. It's brilliant, Imogen. I couldn't see what you meant when you said it, but now I can. It's a lovely idea." She turned to Agnes. "Have you asked the mothers yet?"

Agnes smiled. "No. That's just what I was trying to tell Imogen. I don't know what they'll say. They'll think I'm mad."

Fiona laughed. "I know, but once they see it, they'll understand. I'll come and tell them with you, if you like?" She wiped her hands and they went through into the ward together. There were five women in the ward, one of whom had twins. After some discussion they followed Fiona and Agnes through into the labour ward bringing their babies with them. Their faces clearly showed that they were humouring the crazy 'oberuni' out of good manners.

Agnes spoke to one of them again, taking her hand and holding it out to Imogen as she pointed towards the wall where her own and Fiona's hand-prints stood out clearly. Understanding dawned on the women's faces and Imogen soon had a line of eager hands to paint. It was a little more difficult to manage the babies' prints but with so many willing helpers the task was soon done. The women insisted on adding footprints from their babies too.

"I've left a few spaces for Comfort Atta." Imogen said as they finished up. "I didn't want her to miss out. Do you know where she is? It would be good to get her prints while we still have the paint out."

"She went with Kofi to talk to one of the groups, I think," Fiona answered. "They should be back by now. I'll check down in the clinic."

She was back in a couple of minutes, a bewildered Comfort Atta in tow. "I don't want to paint my hands, Fiona, really, what are you talking about?" She came to a complete stop as she took in the altered labour room, her eyes darting from one to the other of them. "Oh! My goodness." Comfort Atta looked at Imogen incredulously. "You did this in just this afternoon? Wyadee, wyadee paa." Her beaming face made the translation Fiona provided in Imogen's ear unnecessary.

Comfort Atta's prints were added in the spaces Imogen had left and the border was complete. An undulating line of prints circled the walls, large and small in a random sequence. The dark blue stood out clearly against the soft pink background, the overall effect gentle and soothing.

"That's brightened the place up a bit, anyway." Imogen regarded her handiwork with pride.

The three midwives looked at Imogen and moved as one to embrace her. "It's wonderful." Fiona spoke for them all. "We'd never have thought of doing anything like this. Thank you." Imogen blushed a little. "I'm glad you like it," she said simply, beginning to clear away the paint and brushes.

An Abundance of Life

20

Fiona struggled to hold back the tears as she lifted the small lifeless body from the labour room bed. It was the silence she always found so awful. No cry to signal a new arrival, no exclamation of welcoming joy, just a dreadful void created by the absence of one anticipated new life. She looked up towards the head of the bed. The woman's face was still too, eyes closed. It was her fourth child and there had been no indication that anything was amiss until the last few minutes: the baby had shown no sign of life at all. Fiona's fine tuned midwifery instinct warned her that the trouble was not yet over.

She felt the woman's belly again. The placenta should be coming soon. It was almost ten minutes since the baby was born. She turned to Comfort B. "Could you get the ergometrine for me, please," she said quietly, "and bring an infusion set and some fluid, too." She checked the woman's pulse. It was too fast and felt fluttery under her fingers.

"Adjoa, are you feeling any more pains?" Fiona inquired softly in Twi. The woman's eyes flickered open briefly and she shook her head.

Comfort came back into the room with the ergometrine already drawn up into a syringe. Fiona spoke to the woman again. "I'm just going to give you an injection in your leg, Adjoa. Something to help with the afterbirth. OK?" Adjoa hardly reacted to the prick of the needle and Fiona's unease grew stronger. Comfort already had the intravenous infusion pack hung on the stand and was running the fluid through the tubing. Fiona took up Adjoa's hand to check her pulse a second time, and then it happened.

The trickle of blood which had followed the birth of the stillborn baby suddenly became a flood, pouring out of the woman in a torrent. Fiona grabbed a tourniquet from the side bench and wrapped it quickly around Adjoa's arm. She tapped vigorously, trying to raise a vein into which she could insert the intravenous needle. Comfort stood ready with the tubing, also directing the woman's frantic mother in placing a bowl to catch the blood which was cascading off the side of the narrow labour bed.

"Dammit, it must be here." Fiona swore under her breath, her fingers feeling desperately for a vein in the woman's arm. She took the needle from Comfort's hand and pushed into the skin. Relief surged through her as the clear tubing turned red, and she whipped off the tourniquet, turning the drip full on. "Thank god."

She switched her attention and felt Adjoa's stomach again. The placenta had finally appeared, but the woman's stomach was still soft, the empty womb a squishy bulk under Fiona's questing fingers. She massaged it roughly drawing a groan from Adjoa who otherwise lay unmoving. "I'm sorry. I know it hurts." The bleeding went on the same as before. Fiona checked her watch. Only four minutes had passed but it felt far longer. The bowl under the bed was already half full. '*Dear god, please*', she prayed inwardly. "Comfort, could you get another ergometrine, quickly." Fiona's voice was urgent, and Comfort broke into a run as she crossed to the cupboard in the corner of the utility room. Fiona continued with her massage but her fingers told her nothing was changing. The placenta was complete so the haemorrhage was not due to any problem there. The second shot of ergometrine that she gave directly into the intravenous tube also made no difference. The bowl was now almost overflowing onto the floor.

Fiona reached up to Adjoa's neck, feeling for the pulse of the carotid artery. It was barely detectable and she knew the battle was lost, but she kept on trying for several more minutes. When the bleeding finally stopped, it was not as a result of her efforts to stem the flow but because the heart was no longer beating in Adjoa's still body. Fiona bent her head for a moment, raising her eyes to meet those of Adjoa's mother. "I'm so sorry," she whispered.

The woman began the soul-destroying ululating wail that Fiona had heard too many times. Mechanically she noted the time. A little less than half an hour was all it took for a woman's life to ebb away. Adjoa was just twenty six. She felt anger stir in her, welcoming it's heat. The labour room felt cold despite its new coat of cosy pink paint. As she helped Comfort B to clear up she railed inwardly against the stupid waste of human life and against her own inadequacy. It was no comfort to know that even in the most advanced hospitals the same tragedy could still happen. She recalled the obstetrician from her student days who had described post-partum haemorrhage as 'like turning on a tap'. By now, she knew only too well what he meant, recollecting her previous disbelief with a chilled detachment.

As she completed the notes Comfort's hand gripped her shoulder. "You did your best, Sister Fiona, no one could have done more."

"Not now, perhaps, but if she'd had enough to eat, if she wasn't anaemic, if she didn't have to work right up till she delivered, that's when we should have done something. Before she even came anywhere near the labour room." Fiona dropped her head into her hands.

"But it takes time for people to understand all these things, and you know that even if all the women came here for antenatal checks, we still would lose a few like this. Sometimes there is nothing we can do. That is all." Comfort was well named, thought Fiona, raising her head wearily. "I know, Comfort, I know. It's just sometimes it's hard to accept." Fiona put her hand over Comfort's where it still rested on her shoulder.

The death of the woman and baby cast a pall over the compound. It was only mid-morning but already Fiona felt exhausted. *'Pull yourself together',* she told herself fiercely. *'It's not helping anyone to give in to misery. You're just overtired, that's all'.* It was true she'd had two busy nights on call, but she could usually shake off the lack of sleep without difficulty. The house was quiet. Imogen was out with Kofi Paul for the day, catching the maize harvest in one of the nearby villages.

She was picking at her midday meal when the sound of hurrying footsteps approaching the door brought her to her feet. "Could you come to the clinic, Sister Fiona. There's a boy, he's unconscious, I'm not sure why." Kittewaa's voice was urgent.

Fiona followed Kittewaa down to the outpatient building where a small crowd had gathered. A couple of the benches had been pushed together to form a makeshift bed and the boy lay there on his side, his hand hanging limply over one edge. He was about fourteen. Fiona recognised him from one of the youth groups. She took the paper Kittewaa held out to her, noting the observations she'd made: low temperature, slow respiratory rate and no response to stimuli at all. She looked up at the crowd.

"Did anyone come with him?"

After a moment two boys stepped forward, their heads down. Fiona beckoned them closer speaking to them quietly in Twi. "Can you tell us what happened, how long he's been like this?" The boys shuffled their feet uncomfortably, remaining silent. "You're from Nsupa, aren't you? That's quite a distance. How did you get here?" Fiona kept her voice calm. It was clear the boys knew something. They'd probably been up to something they shouldn't have been, she thought, and tried again.

"It's OK. I just want to know what happened to him, when did he become sick and how long he's been unconscious. You don't have to tell me anything else."

The younger looking boy spoke in a whisper. "We were in the bush, Sister. All night. On my uncle's farm." His eyes flicked up to hers and away again. "We were drinking, Sister. Akpeteshie. He hadn't drunk it before. He didn't wake up this morning, so we brought him here."

Akpeteshie was a local alcoholic drink, distilled from palm wine. It was almost one hundred percent proof as far as Fiona knew, and the purity varied from one still to another. Bending closer to the unconscious boy, she caught the characteristically sweet smell on his breath. Her heart sank. "Do you know how much he drank?" she asked, still softly.

The boy nodded, his face miserable. "The others dared him, Sister. I told him 'no' but he didn't listen. He drank a whole bottle." He wiped his eyes furtively, unwilling to let the other boy see he was crying.

"Jesus." Fiona swore softly, thinking fast. "Has he vomited at all?" The boy shook his head. She had no experience of alcohol poisoning but the boy's chances were not looking good. "OK, thank you for telling me what happened. I think we need to get him to hospital. Does he have any relatives living in Osubuso?" she asked. The boy in front of her nodded and sniffed. "His auntie, Sister."

"Can you go and ask her to come? Tell her she needs to go to the hospital with him. You know where she lives?" The boy nodded again and set off at a trot. Fiona drew Kittewaa to one side where they could not be heard. "It doesn't look too good, I'm afraid. I think he's got alcohol poisoning. He's been unconscious all night by the sound of it. He feels quite cold, so cover him with a blanket. Can you send someone into town to see if any of the taxis are willing to take him to Afafranto? Kofi Paul has the Patrol and Kofi took the truck to a youth group meeting. They won't be back till this evening." Kittewaa bobbed her head briefly indicating she understood. "In the meantime keep him as quiet as possible and on his side like he is now. OK? I'll be up at the house, I need to write a referral letter."

She had just finished the letter when the wailing told her it would not be needed. Reluctantly she went back down to the clinic building where she found the boy's parents had arrived just in time to watch him die. She explained what she knew of the circumstances to his father, who listened gravely. "Thank you, Sister. We knew when he did not come home last night that he was in trouble. Thank you for your care. I know you have done all you could."

Fiona took the man's outstretched hand, her throat aching as she saw the grief in his face. The boy's mother also turned to thank her for her help. "I'm very sorry we couldn't do more." Fiona managed to say, overwhelmed by this generosity in the midst of such sorrow. She stayed a few minutes longer and then made her way back up to the house.

She sank into a chair and laid her head back, letting the tears flow freely for a while. Another young life thrown away.

When she heard the running footsteps for a third time, Fiona felt dully resigned to the inevitable. This time it was a two year old child with severe fitting which neither a chloroquine injection nor anti- convulsants could stop. She died within an hour. Her father stood before Fiona asking repeatedly in an agonised voice, "What should we do, Sister, please tell me. We have had three children and all have died. Why has this happened to us?" Fiona could offer him no comfort. She was drained of all emotion, merely an empty shell, a robot. For the remainder of the afternoon her actions were purely automatic. She did not even summon the energy to be angry when Kofi returned with news that he had broken the portable whiteboard on the way back from his trip to the youth group.

Late in the afternoon she sat on the back verandah, unmoving and unseeing. Some part of her mind registered the return of a vehicle and the opening of the door, but she did not move. Imogen came over and squatted beside her chair taking a listless hand in her own and chafing it. "Comfort Atta told me you've had a rotten day. I'm sorry. I wish I'd been here. Is there anything I can do?"

"Help me pack." Fiona's voice was dull and expressionless. "I might as well go home now for all the good I'm doing here."

"Oh, Fiona, don't say that. You know it's not true." Imogen fought to keep her own emotion under control, shaken to see Fiona in such despair. "It's been a terrible day, I know, but you're doing tremendous work here, you know you are."

"Really? I hadn't noticed." Fiona's sarcasm was directed inwards. "People are dying more successfully, is that it? And I can't even get the staff to act responsibly. Did you know Kofi broke the whiteboard today? Our only piece of expensive educational equipment. He tied it on to the back of the truck, but didn't notice the rope was badly frayed in two places, so it fell off and broke halfway home." Fiona laughed bitterly. "It's hopeless. A total waste of effort."

Imogen reached her arms around Fiona, holding her close. "I know it seems that way just now, but that's not the real picture. Just think of the things I've seen since I came. The project is creating a real force for change, you know it is. The women's co-ops are wonderfully successful. The work Kofi Paul is doing with the farmers is improving productivity, slowly, I grant you, but very surely. The youth groups provide a focus for kids in lots of the villages."

"The boy today, he belonged to one of our youth groups. Didn't help him much, did it?" Fiona refused to be comforted. "And the woman who died, she came here to the clinic in good time, expecting us to look after her. I never even spotted anything wrong with her. And for the little girl it was already too late."

Imogen shook her gently. "Three deaths in one day is hard for anyone to cope with. But the clinic does save lives, too, and help people to stay healthy, you can't deny the good that you all do, Fiona."

"But what difference does it make overall?" Fiona looked at Imogen blankly, "OK, there's an odd life saved here or there, but look how many are still dying. It's pathetic." She snorted derisively. "You know what that little girl's father said to me today? Do we have to go on having children just to watch them die? That's the kind of service we offer, a place to bring your dying children."

"Of course, it's especially dreadful when children die. But some people are alive today only because you and the others are here. Think of those malnourished children who were in the clinic when I was here in April. You enabled them to stay alive until the harvest and now they're strong again. What was it, one hundred and fifty, I think you said there'd been. That's something to set against the three deaths today, surely."

Two tears rolled down Fiona's cheeks. "I know you're right, Imogen. It just all seems so pointless today. It's like one step forward and two steps back." She made an effort to recover control. "And I don't know why I'm feeling so over-emotional and sorry for myself. It's not like I'm the one that's suffering. I don't know what's the matter with me."

Imogen reached out a gentle finger and wiped the tears from Fiona's cheek. "You're working far too hard, that's all. When did you last have a real break? I mean, have you actually taken a holiday since you got here?" Her gentle reproof raised a faint flicker of a smile, although Fiona's eyes remained closed.

"I had two weeks off at Christmas." Fiona said, drawing in a shaky breath. "And I've been down to Accra a couple of times since."

"See what I mean." Imogen took hold of her hands again. "You're off-duty this weekend, aren't you? And you're not on-call until Thursday, is that right?" Seeing Fiona's slight nod, she continued, "Well then, you're going to take a proper break with me. Get right away from here for five days. Recharge your batteries, have a bit of rest and recreation."

"You've still got a lot to do for your book, and not much time left. You can't afford to take time off just because I'm being pathetic," Fiona rolled her head slowly from side to side in protest.

"And you can't afford not to." Imogen was adamant. "I can change my flight back, go a bit later. It won't make any difference to me, but a little holiday will make all the difference to you. No argument. I already told Agnes and Comfort Atta."

Fiona opened her eyes at that. "You cheeky sod. I suppose you've booked a hotel somewhere too?"

Imogen patted her arm, absurdly relieved to see even this slight evidence of a return to a more familiar Fiona. "No, I haven't, but only because I had no idea where we could go."

"I do know a little place down on the beach, near to Cape Coast." Fiona was warming to the idea. "A few days beside the sea with nothing to do would be heavenly, wouldn't it?"

"Perfect. I thought you might know the right place." Imogen stood up. "Now you just stay there while I get some supper for us both. How long does it take to get to Cape Coast?"

"About four, maybe four and a half hours usually."

"Good, then you can get off to bed straight after you've eaten. You'll have time to pack in the morning."

<u>21</u>

Walking back from the telephone booth in the town just after eight the next morning Imogen felt very pleased. Changing the ticket was easier than she expected and she was now booked on a flight for the twenty-fourth. That gave her ten days longer, more than enough, she was sure. Waking early, she had intercepted Esther in the kitchen. "Don't wake Fiona today, Esther. She needs a bit more sleep after yesterday." Esther acted as their alarm clock each morning, bringing a cup of tea to each bedroom. She looked at Imogen, her face full of concern. "She works so hard, Sister Imogen, and she cares so much."

"I know, Esther, so we'll just let her sleep a bit longer today, alright." Imogen took her own cup of tea from Esther's hand. "I'll have this on the verandah, thanks."

Fiona finally emerged from her room about ten o'clock and came to join Imogen where she was scribbling at the table. Imogen looked up. Fiona's face had lost the dreadful strain which had worried her so the previous night. "Are you feeling a bit better?"

"Yes, thanks." Fiona stretched. "Ooh, I haven't had such a

good sleep in ages, and I can't remember getting up so late since I don't know when." She smiled at Imogen.

"You needed it. You push yourself too hard."

Fiona's face took on a rueful expression. "I know, but I can't help myself. There's always so much to do." She rested her hand briefly on Imogen's shoulder. "Thanks for being there last night, Imogen, I needed someone to buck me up again."

Imogen reached up and took her hand, pressing it lightly. "I didn't do anything, really." She felt a fluttering in her stomach as she looked at Fiona, but tried to ignore it. "Now, you better get packed. We'll need to be leaving in a while."

Fiona's face lit up with a smile, "Ooh, a real holiday, I can't wait." She hugged her arms tightly around herself. "But I just have to sort a few things out first. I promise I won't be too long."

Imogen felt the buzz of anticipation increase. "Alright, but two o'clock is the latest. Any later than that and I'll just kidnap you. Understood?"

The drive down towards Cape Coast went smoothly. Almost as soon as they left the compound, just before two, Fiona felt her spirits rising. "Let's have a bit of music, hey?" she said to Imogen, pointing to the jumbled heap of tapes under the dash. Imogen shuffled through them and selected one, passing it over for Fiona to put into the machine. By chance, the mix of Rod Stewart, Fleetwood Mac, and the Eagles was one of Fiona's favourites. With the turn of a switch "Maggie May" belted out at top volume. Fiona knew all the lyrics and sang along through the tape, uncaring whether she was in tune or not.

She was heading for a small hotel just to the west of Cape Coast with a magnificent view of Elmina Castle. That was a spooky place close up, but from a distance it looked wonderful. She hoped they'd be able to get a cabin near the beach. She always found the sound of the sea so restful, and having agreed to this break she was now impatient to arrive.

Momentarily she let herself feel guilty about taking Imogen away from her assignment. One look was enough to reassure her. Imogen was absorbed in the scenery. Her features were relaxed, she even sang along here and there, without Fiona's gusto but more tunefully. '*And it was her suggestion, after all, so just stop it, you old worry-guts.*' Fiona gave in to the joy of release from responsibility.

It was getting on towards evening when she turned off the main road and into the hotel compound. The first impression could not have been better with the sun dropping down over the sea in a haze and dark purple-grey thunder clouds massed back over the land, reflecting a yellow light into the sky. Fiona turned off the engine. "Will this do?" she asked Imogen.

"It's fantastic. When you said a little place by the beach I thought you meant a shack. This is amazing." Imogen took in her surroundings. The main hotel building was to their left with graceful thatched verandahs all around. Behind and to the right she could see a swimming pool, its slatted wooden surround dotted with sun-loungers and umbrellas. Individual accommodation cabins, also thatched, were spaced around a large compound. All in all it offered a perfect mixture of sociability and privacy.

At the registration desk the clerk was extremely helpful. "Yes, madam. We have one vacant cabin down by the shore. It's a deluxe double. Or there is a tourist twin cabin nearer to the pool. Which would you like to take?"

Fiona looked at Imogen, not wishing to make any assumptions. Imogen simply raised an eyebrow, "You choose," she said.

"Oh, hang the expense. Let's have the one by the sea, Imogen. It's worth it just to get the breeze and hear the surf in the night." The other implications of Fiona's choice remained unspoken.

From the outside the cabins looked traditional, but this was in fact a clever disguise. Underneath the thatch was a solidly built unit, with hot and cold running water in the bathroom, reading lamps, a large double bed with overhanging mosquito net, and two comfortable armchairs. At the back was a screened in verandah with more deep cushioned cane chairs. Power was supplied by solar panels discreetly positioned on the roof of each cabin.

"Perfect." Imogen said, sitting in one of the armchairs and examining the room. "There's even a minibar. This is a deluxe cabin."

"Stuff that." Fiona was undoing the buttons of her shirt and wriggling out of her trousers. "It's the shower I want. I haven't had a hot one in months. You can get very, very tired of bucket baths." Grabbing her toilet bag she disappeared into the bathroom.

Imogen took a cold Star beer from the fridge and sat on the verandah watching the sun drop into the sea. The price of the cabin was a little on the high side, but she'd spent hardly any of her moderate expense allowance so far. She wanted this to be her treat. She smiled as Fiona's voice floated out from the bathroom over the splashing of the water. It was a revelation to see her in such a carefree mood.

It was dark by the time Fiona came out of the shower. For a moment Imogen was bemused; who was this woman with the long, thick, chestnut brown hair? "Wow." she exclaimed. "I've never seen you with your hair down. It's beautiful."

Fiona accepted the compliment without comment. "Sorry I was such an age, I just couldn't bring myself to get out. But there's plenty of water here. When you've had yours, can we get something to eat? I'm starving."

The food was simple but good. A mix of Ghanaian, European and Middle Eastern dishes. "There's a strong Lebanese connection, here." Fiona explained. They decided to pause before considering the dessert menu. Imogen went to use the toilet. Watching her walk back to the table, Fiona suddenly understood the reason for her own high spirits, her singing in the shower. Her eyes did not leave Imogen's as she came the last few yards and sat down.

"What is it? Have I left something open?" Imogen could not look away to check her clothing, so compelling was Fiona's gaze.

"Will you come to bed with me?"

"I was sort of assuming I would, given that there is only the one. But I suppose I could sleep in the chair, if you insist." Imogen smiled easily as she spoke, enjoying the sensations Fiona's simple proposition aroused.

"No. I mean right now."

Imogen hardly hesitated, her heart suddenly beating faster. "Yes, of course. Is that what you want?"

Fiona nodded dumbly and stood up. As they walked the short distance back to the cabin she was acutely aware of everything around her. The surf broke repetitively in the distance, hissing up the beach in little crescendoes, with an occasional louder thump and whoosh. The wind lifted the leaves of the coconut palms clattering them together like an uncoordinated percussion band. The constant singing whirr of cicadas added to the exotic symphony. Above her head a crescent moon suffused the night sky with a silvery luminescence, while beneath her feet the sandy path scrunched with each step. The tangy salt air filled her lungs, so different from the earthy smells of Osubuso. Her skin was on fire.

Imogen opened the cabin door and stepped through into the darkness of the room. Fiona caught her hand as she reached for the light switch. "No." She kicked the door closed and leaning back against it pulled Imogen hard against her, running her hands up under her shirt to cup her breasts, her thumbs brushing across taut nipples.

"I want you." Fiona's voice held an undercurrent of desperation. Imogen's eager response to searching lips and tongue gave her answer.

22

"Sorry about the noise. I couldn't help it." Fiona apologised softly, a while later, as she lay in Imogen's embrace. The netting swayed gently above them in the breeze from the open louvre windows.

"Don't be. I like passionate women." Imogen squeezed her still closer. "And I don't suppose anyone else heard. They're probably still waiting for their coffees back there in the restaurant." Her teasing was tender.

"I didn't exactly notice you hanging back, Miss Prim." Fiona moved to straddle Imogen, looking down at her jauntily. "It's very womb-like in here isn't it?" she said, indicating the netting which enclosed the bed.

"Mmmm." Imogen was distracted by Fiona's hair, hanging loosely instead of confined in its usual barrette. She ran her fingers through it repeatedly, savouring the springiness. Fiona lowered her head, sweeping her hair tantalisingly back and forth over Imogen's nipples. It was a long time before anything of real coherence was said.

They slept late into the morning. Fiona awoke first and enticed Imogen into wakefulness with feather- soft kisses.

Eventually they made their way back to the restaurant for a late, leisurely lunch, watching the life of the hotel go on around them.

"Fancy a dip in the pool?"

"You know I do." Fiona dropped her voice to a low growl.

"I meant the swimming pool." Imogen smiled.

Throughout the afternoon they giggled over double meanings. "You're making me all wet." Imogen complained as Fiona stood beside her and shook herself after a cooling dip. "You're so slippery," from Fiona as she rubbed sun lotion into the backs of Imogen's thighs. Trying to be sensible Fiona said, "We shouldn't stay out too long, you'll get burned." "But I thought we were being very discreet and not 'out' at all." was Imogen's quick response.

Their hilarity was only increased by the puzzled looks they were drawing from other people around the pool and eventually they retreated to the cabin intending to calm down.

Their second night together was as tumultuous as the first and by mid-afternoon of the following day Imogen was exhausted. The combination of lack of sleep, the unaccustomed heat, and sun and sea air were taking their toll. She suggested a siesta. Within seconds of lying down she was deeply asleep.

Fiona left Imogen sleeping and took a book out onto the verandah, settling into the comfortable cushions of a cane chair. But the book remained unopened as fear and desire waged a battle in her head, her mind adrift in memories of Miranda's double accusations of excess and neglect.

"Penny for them." Fiona jumped. Imogen was standing in the doorway wearing only a T-shirt which was almost long enough to be respectable should anyone pass. She came and sat on Fiona's knee. "What are you looking so serious about?"

A slight colour rose under Fiona's tanned cheeks and her answer was only a partial truth. "I was just reflecting on my selfishness. I haven't exactly tried to control myself in the last two days." The feel of Imogen's naked legs against her was already undermining any such good intentions.

"What's this?" Imogen turned Fiona's face toward her. "Don't be silly. You don't need to apologise for wanting me, you idiot."

"But you're exhausted. And you're not used to the heat, and the sun or anything."

"Fiona, listen to me. I love your passion, the abundance of your body, how we are together. Yes, I'm a little tired, but that's all. I want you just as much."

"I just feel I've overwhelmed you a bit, bulldozed you along." Fiona's concerned expression did not change.

"Have I complained? No. And I'm not likely to, either." A wicked gleam came into Imogen's eye. "Although, on second thoughts, there is one thing ...."

Fiona regarded her with suspicion. "What's that?"

"Well, it's just, you know as a lesbian I never thought I'd hear myself say this, but do you mind sleeping on the wet patch tonight?" She laughed uproariously as Fiona, her face flaming, tried to take revenge by tickling.

Eventually, they calmed themselves enough to go and eat supper. The following morning Fiona was determined that they should get out of the hotel compound at least.

"Look, we've only got a couple more days here, so we are going to do some sightseeing today. OK?" Fiona's voice was fierce as she caught Imogen's hand firmly in her own, preventing it from completing its journey downwards. "Behave yourself."

Imogen laughed up at her from where she lay. "You're so funny when you try and scold. Alright, alright. I'm coming." She leapt off the bed as Fiona moved menacingly towards her feet. "No tickling, I give in."

As they climbed into the car Imogen asked "So, what am I being taken to see?"

"First of all, there's a little pottery place in Winneba which I thought you might find interesting, then we have to go and see the castle."

"The what?" Imogen looked bewildered.

"Elmina Castle." Fiona pointed as they pulled out of the hotel compound. "That's it over there."

"Oh, I see. I've been wondering what it was. When you said 'castle' I couldn't work it out. I don't associate castles with Africa."

"It was built by Europeans," Fiona explained, "during the slave trade. It's not exactly a light-hearted touristy place, but it is important to see it." She swerved to avoid a pothole at the last minute. "Whoops, sorry about that, some of them are hard to spot."

The drive to Winneba took about an hour. They pulled up in a dusty street with large storm drains on either side. Piles of cement bags lay at intervals along the narrow uneven pavement indicating the ongoing construction work. In front of them was a large shop front window, behind which were stacks of pottery.

Inside, Imogen pored over the pots, lingering particularly at one range. The simple earthenware pots were topped with an inch or so of delicately woven basket-work. "These are lovely, aren't they?" She moved on through the shop, stopping again at a table displaying brightly coloured mugs. These were roughly glazed, each one decorated with a different symbol of some sort. Imogen looked at Fiona inquiringly. "What are these? Do they have some significance?"

"They're adinkra symbols, sort of visual proverbs is how I think of them. You see them on cloth too, traditionally navy and white. You may have seen it in the market in Afafranto?"

"Oh yes, I think so. The symbols weren't as clear as these though." She moved towards the back of the shop and was soon deep in a technical discussion with the proprietor about the types of clay, glazes and other processes used.

Fiona leant against a table content to observe. It seemed Imogen's slight body was hardly still for a moment. '*Except when she's behind a camera*', Fiona mused, '*she's quite different then, almost immobile, all her attention focused on the image in the viewfinder*'. Aware that she had probably passed a point of no return in her feelings toward Imogen, she pushed away the anticipation of the pain that would surely follow.

Imogen came over to her. "It's very interesting to hear how he does his work. Do you mind if I have a quick look at the kilns and stuff? I don't want to keep you hanging around if you're bored, but ..."

Fiona smiled indulgently. "What do you think I brought you here for, stupid? Go on, take as long as you want. I'm quite happy being mindless for a while. Don't worry about me." She smiled at the potter, exchanging greetings in Twi before the two of them left her.

When Imogen returned, Fiona was sitting on the pavement playing cat's cradle with a small girl. She got up slowly and stretched, bidding the child goodbye. They got back into the car. "Did you find out all you wanted to know?"

"Mmmm," Imogen was busy scribbling in her notebook. "Just a min. I want to get it down before I forget." She finished writing after a moment and looked at Fiona. "Yes, I did, thanks. It was fascinating. It's given me something to think about." She looked about her eagerly. "So what next?"

"Well, I thought maybe a bite of lunch and then the castle. It's better to go around it a bit later. It's very hot inside in the middle of the day. Keep your eyes peeled for a likely chop-bar." She concentrated on the road for a while.

They ate kenkey and light soup at a small chop-bar which appealed to Imogen because of its name; 'God Feeds All Chop Bar' the sign announced proudly. "Well, I suppose that saves the cook a lot of trouble then." Imogen laughed, "come on, we have to try it." Fiona could never quite decide whether she liked kenkey, with its sour, fermented taste, or not.

It was about three when they parked alongside the imposing whitewashed walls of Elmina Castle and made their way over the narrow causeway to the interior. "You might find it a bit upsetting," Fiona warned Imogen. "I did the first time I came here. We can go out again if it gets too much." Imogen nodded, although she could not see what was upsetting about a building.

The guide took them around the interior, pointing out its various features in a pleasant voice which belied the obscenity of what he described. There was the condemned cell in which they were imprisoned in complete darkness for a couple of seconds; the large building in the centre of the courtyard which had been church, soldiers' mess hall and slave market, including the cubby-hole from which the purchasers could examine the goods without fear of contamination; and a long narrow tunnel leading down to the harbour. "This was the exit to the transport ships," the guide explained. "The sea was a lot higher then, so the ships could dock right outside here. The slaves went straight from this passage into the ship's hold, almost without seeing the light of day. Then they were taken off to sea." In another part of the castle, high on the roof was the room in which a captive Asantahene, King of the Ashanti, spent the last years of his life in exile.

But it was the area below the commandant's quarters which caused Imogen to finally give in to her growing sense of horror. It was a small courtyard sunk down within several layers of surrounding balconies. Not much light came in, especially as it was now well into late afternoon. The commandant's quarters were directly above them, spreading back from the first floor balcony. They had already seen the rather spacious rooms earlier in the tour. Now they stood at the bottom of a steep little stair which led down into this yard. Sunk into the floor diagonally opposite were two cannon balls and behind them the door to the female slaves' quarters. This was a square room, not more than fifteen feet each side into which, the guide informed them, were regularly packed about two hundred women.

"When the commandant wanted entertainment, he would call for one of the women," the guide was saying, his voice still completely matter of fact. "The men would bring out a woman, strip her and chain her to those cannon balls and he would decide whether to take her for the night or not."

The image was stark in Imogen's mind: the commandant arrogant on the balcony, hips thrust forward, twisting his moustache as he leered down into the courtyard assessing the slave below him; and the woman, perhaps newly arrived having had god knows what terrible journey, standing, her legs splayed apart between the two cannon balls. Imogen felt terror flood through her as she imagined the woman's predicament.

"Get me out of here, Fiona." She gripped her lover's hand tightly, squeezing her eyes shut against the tears which threatened to overwhelm her.

Fiona led her back out of the castle and into the mellowing afternoon sunshine. They sat silently under the castle walls and watched the waves crashing onto the shore. Behind them the little harbour was bright and bustling, every boat with a random combination of different national flags fluttering at its masthead in a display of internationalism. The air was heavy with the smell of fish drifting across from the circular smoke-ovens on the roadside a little beyond the harbour.

Eventually Imogen spoke. "I couldn't bear it. It's as if I could see them all, hear them screaming and crying." She looked at Fiona, still clearly shocked. "I'm sorry, you must think me pathetic."

"No. That's exactly how I reacted when I first came here. I tried to warn you, but it is hard to imagine until you're inside." Fiona held her close. "It's me who should be apologising for bringing you here when I knew it would upset you."

"I'm glad you did, in a horrible sort of way. It's important to see it, to understand a little of what was done in the name of civilisation. And the guide," Imogen's voice broke again, "how can he even talk to us when that's his own people's history he's describing, never mind in such an undramatic way. Why are any of them nice to us at all? I'd want to spit on us if I were a Ghanaian."

"You're not personally responsible, Imogen," Fiona answered soberly, "but I agree it's hard not to feel that way. And we're still just as arrogant, really. Thinking we've always got the right answers and the right to apply them. It makes me feel uncomfortable to be a part of any so-called development project."

"I know, but people like you do such a lot of good, too. Noone would describe the way you relate to the people here as arrogant, but . . . I don't know what I think any more."

"I talked about it with Kofi once, and he had a different angle. He said, for Ghana the slave trade was important because of what *didn't* happen here, maybe how development was stalled or distorted. He said it's hard to know the impact of an absence. And the people who stayed were never slaves. He thought that made a difference, but I don't know. I just end up thinking the same thing; that we all have to do what we can to make amends, however little and however futile it seems." She stood up and pulled Imogen to her feet. "Anyway, we can't solve all the world's problems, just we two, can we?"

"No, I suppose you're right. All we can do is to make sure we don't make things worse, if we can help it." Imogen sighed deeply. "Come on then, let's get back to the hotel. I've had a big enough dose of reality for today."

23

They took things easy on their final day. In the early morning, before it became hot, they strolled along the beach, hand in hand, dodging the breakers along the sea's edge.

"It's a shame it's not possible to swim in it," Imogen said. "It looks so inviting."

"I know, but the undercurrents are vicious. They've had several drownings over the years when people have ignored the warnings. I'm quite happy to stick with looking at the sea from a safe distance. Let's stop a while." Fiona pulled Imogen down to sit against the trunk of a coconut palm. She ran handfuls of sand through her fingers, watching the way it fell.

An hour or so passed in idle chat, with Imogen trying to learn a few words of Twi. So far all she could manage was one standard phrase meaning 'I don't understand Twi - Me nti Twi', which sounded like 'minty tree'. "It makes me think of a bush with Fox's glacier mints hanging from the branches." Imogen giggled. They gave up when the subtleties of the tonal pronunciation proved too much.

Wandering back to the hotel, they spent until lunch time lounging round the pool with long, cold drinks and ice-cream. In the heat of the early afternoon they retreated inside the cabin and made love slowly, then fell asleep, legs entwined under the cooling draught of the ceiling fan.

Imogen woke before Fiona. She pulled herself into a sitting position and studied her lover's body as it lay relaxed in sleep. Her skin was tanned a rich honey-gold from their days in the sun, darker where her arms and legs were continually exposed. Freckles seemed to have multiplied a hundredfold in the last few days, spreading over every inch of skin. The swell of her breasts was mirrored in the curve of her belly, the swoop over her hips. An idea began to form in Imogen's mind, her gaze changed from lover to that of an artist at work. "I wonder if she'd let me ..."

"Let you what?" Fiona spoke making Imogen startle. "You wonder if I'll let you what?"

"Oh, nothing, I didn't realise you were awake." Imogen blushed. "You'll probably just think I'm even weirder than you do already if I tell you."

Fiona chuckled delightedly. "My, my. What little secret perversities have you been hiding from me? I'm quite adventurous you know. You can tell me what you want." She rolled around catching Imogen's foot and putting her teeth to the soft skin of the instep. "What's your fetish, miss? Come on, out with it."

"Stop it." Imogen tried to maintain her dignity. "It's nothing like that. I just want to take some photos of you naked, that's all." She saw how Fiona's face sobered sharply and hurried on. "It's not what you think, honest. I don't mean full frontal or anything like that."

Fiona observed her warily. "I should hope not. I wouldn't dream of anything so pornographic, but if it's more artistic you might persuade me."

"There's just some angles and curves, particular elements that make up your body I wanted to try and capture, that's all, something I wanted to try and do, but it doesn't matter."

The idea of her body as artistic inspiration was a novel one to Fiona, and intriguing. "Tell me about it. Explain what elements."

"I don't know if I can, really, it's all a bit vague at the moment." Imogen paused thoughtfully. "I suppose it's a sort of portrait, but an unconventional one. Not a single picture but a collection, building up into a whole."

"What do I have to do?" Fiona flung back an arm and raised one leg, deliberately provocative now she knew Imogen was serious. "Is this how you'd want me?" She pursed her lips in a mock kiss.

"Not exactly, no, or at least not for the photos," Imogen smiled warmly. "And if I'm going to do them, it has to be soon, while there's still enough light. Are you really willing?"

"I'm flattered," Fiona said simply. "Go ahead, you just tell me what to do and I'll try my best."

Imogen fetched the camera from her bag, fiddling about with her film and lenses, adjusting the blinds for the best light, before she was ready. She concentrated on separate portions of Fiona's body, as she'd said, catching the way the light fell and shadows formed. First the angles of shoulder, elbows, knee, then the softer swells of belly, breast and thigh, intimate places such as ear lobes, the crease of a buttock or the nape of her neck. Gradually she built up a jigsaw of images. Other than issuing instructions "lift your arm higher" or "can you twist a little more to the right?" she was silent, the only sound the click and whirr of the camera.

Imogen's gaze was both intimate and distant, the camera transforming her from lover to professional. Now and then she touched Fiona to hold her steady or emphasise an instruction and her touch too was a mix of the familiar and the impersonal. Fiona felt strangely aroused by the experience.

At last Imogen seemed satisfied, taking the camera strap from around her neck and placing it back in the bag. "Thank you." She returned to Fiona bending to kiss her in gratitude. Fiona pulled her closer hungrily. Imogen resisted, holding back to look at her lover with interest. "Well, I never would have thought it," she exclaimed softly, "you enjoyed it, didn't you? You little harlot." A throaty laugh broke from her as Fiona blushed furiously under her speculative gaze. "You're adorably insatiable." And she sank down into Fiona's embrace.

24

Imogen walked back to the cabin feeling a little guilty. She should have discussed the payment of the bill with Fiona, she knew, but it was easier just to pay it. Fiona was funny when it came to hospitality. She pushed open the cabin door, relieved to hear Fiona still in the shower. At least she didn't have to confront her just yet.

She was sitting in one of the cane chairs watching the stately single-sail boats pulling out from Elmina when Fiona came up behind her a while later. "It's been such a lovely time here, hasn't it?" Fiona nuzzled her ear, reaching her arms round her. "Thanks for suggesting it. When I'm working I always forget how important it is to get away now and then."

Imogen smiled up at her. "Oh, you've tied your hair up again. I like it so much better loose." The rich springy hair was now tightly confined in its customary twist at the nape of Fiona's neck. Imogen stroked it regretfully.

"Are you all set, then? We better go and pay up." Fiona pulled her to her feet.

"I already did."

"Oh. Well, I suppose I did take a long time in the shower." Fiona grinned at her. "What was the damage?" She reached for her wallet.

"My treat," said Imogen.

"Imogen, don't be silly. I can't let you do that. Come on, how much is my share?" Fiona still held her wallet and there was a determined look to the set of her chin but Imogen had her own streak of obstinacy.

"It's my treat," she repeated. "In return for all the hospitality you've already provided."

"But I can't let you do that. Not after I chose the deluxe cabin. I'd never have done that if I thought you would insist on paying. Imogen, let me pay half, it doesn't feel right this way." A slight colour rose under Fiona's cheeks and her green eyes had a hard edge.

"Put your money away, Fiona, I mean it." Imogen tried to keep her voice calm but she could feel her temper rising at Fiona's insistence. They stood confronting one another in the middle of the cabin. Imogen took a deep breath and let her shoulders drop. "I don't want this to spoil everything, please. Just let me do this one thing. Think of it as my contribution to your housekeeping. You've hardly let me give you anything in Osubuso, and you know I've got a reasonable allowance from ActionFirst. I've hardly spent any of it and I'm not taking it home." She took Fiona's hands in hers, squeezing them gently. "Please. Me pa wo kyew."

The use of the traditional Ghanaian phrase tipped the balance in her favour. Fiona gave her hands an answering squeeze. "OK, you win," then bent to pick up the bags.

A few hours later Imogen looked at Fiona cautiously as she pulled over into a space at the edge of the road. The drive had been a quiet one and now they were nearly back in Osubuso. She waited tensely, aware that Fiona had been building up to something for most of the journey.

Fiona turned toward her. "Imogen, before we get home, I have to say something and I'm not quite sure how."

Imogen's heart sank as she anticipated the brush off she felt sure was coming, but she said "Probably best just to spit it straight out, then."

Fiona took a deep breath. "It's not what you're thinking, you know, so don't look so petrified. It's just that things will be different back here in Osubuso."

"How come you can read me like a book, and I can't make out what you think at all?" Imogen reached over and stroked her cheek. "Go on. Tell me what's eating at you."

"The last few days have been wonderful but I can't carry on like that here. For a start I'll be back on duty for three nights tomorrow and I'll need my sleep." Fiona looked directly at Imogen, "I might wish I didn't have to work, but I do, and so do you."

"I know, we'll have to be a bit more restrained, that's all." Imogen said understandingly.

"It's not just that. I know when I'm working I find it hard to focus on anything else. I'm not very good at putting work and a love life together." Fiona's embarrassment at having to put her fears into words brought a slight colour to her cheeks, "You've seen how obsessive I can get."

"I certainly have, on both counts." The memory brought a warm glow into her eyes. "Are you trying to tell me I'll have to sleep in my own bed?"

"Well, yes, that's part of it, I suppose. I know it's daft, but I wouldn't feel comfortable." Fiona looked away from the puzzlement in Imogen's eyes. She made another effort to warn Imogen. "It's just I know what will happen from the moment we get back on the compound: my attention has to be one hundred percent back on the project. I can't be worrying about what's going on between us."

"I see," replied Imogen not really seeing at all, "I had the impression you could cope with more than one thing at once, somehow." She meant to tease but couldn't keep a slight edge from her voice.

"Please, Imogen. It's important to me to get this straight before we get home." Part of Fiona's mind registered that the downward spiral had already begun. What was it Imogen had said, after a couple of weeks some insurmountable barrier always appeared, well here it was already, well ahead of schedule.

Seeing the tension in Fiona's body, Imogen reassured her quickly. "OK, whatever you say." She reached over pulling her close for a kiss, which Fiona broke away from. "Not here, someone could be passing."

Imogen gave a regretful chuckle, "I begin to see what you mean, now." Fiona managed to look both apologetic and unrepentant at the same time. "That's what I'm trying to tell you, Imogen. We have to be very discreet now we're back in Osubuso, not like the last few days at all. Please?" Her voice was pleading.

"OK, I get the message, I'll behave myself with the proper decorum." She smiled to show no offence was taken or intended, and Fiona restarted the car.

25

Over the next couple of days Imogen completed her work with the Ghanaian staff. Now the only part left was the inclusion of Fiona and her role at Osubuso. Today she was hoping to get some shots of the maternity work. The ones she'd taken on the April trip did not have quite the same feel as the work she was doing now with the Ghanaians and she was reluctant to use them in the book. Those first photos of Fiona bathing the resuscitated baby were not ones Imogen wanted to share with a wider public.

Since their return to the project Fiona seemed to have forgotten about Cape Coast altogether. She became completely immersed in her work. '*I suppose she did try to warn me, but I never expected such a complete reverse*'. Imogen reflected wryly. Even with the warning it was a difficult adjustment to make. Apart from meal times, they had hardly spent more than half an hour alone together. Two busy on-call nights were no help, although at least that meant there were now plenty of women and babies in the ward.

Knowing Fiona was still uncomfortable with the idea of featuring in the book, Imogen tried to work out the best way of proceeding. "I want you to forget I'm here at all," she said, reflecting silently that Fiona seemed to have no trouble with this anyway. "You just get on with whatever you're doing and I'll try to interfere as little as possible. It worked well with the others. I'm good at fading into the background."

"I'll try," Fiona replied, "but I sort of seize up when I see the lens pointing at me."

"Well then, perhaps you should talk to me about what you're doing to keep your mind off the camera. You know, explain the routines and such like. I don't know much about midwifery and it will help me pick up on things." Gallantly Imogen did not remind her of a very different reaction to the camera.

"OK. Yes. That's a good idea. It'll help me keep focused on the work, won't it?" Fiona looked happier as they made their way over to the ward. "Right, well, the first thing I do is go round and check all the mums and babies to make sure they're alright, you know, not too much bleeding, no sore bits, babies feeding properly and no infected cords." Fiona preceded her into the ward, still talking. "We've got a little one in just now, born three days ago. He's just a bit over a kilo in weight so we're keeping a very close eye on him."

Imogen watched as Fiona made her round of the eight women in the ward. Initially she did not take many photos, wanting to get a better sense of Fiona's role compared to Agnes and Comfort Atta before she chose her shots. She knew the routine would be repeated so there was little danger of missing anything vital. It gave Fiona a chance to settle, and them both time to get used to being in such close proximity again, albeit in very different circumstances.

"This is the little one," Fiona said, lifting a tiny baby from one of the cots.

"Why the woolly hat?" asked Imogen, thinking the baby looked like a doll with the blue knitted cap covering his head and tied under his chin.

"He needs to keep warm, being so small. See, we've got a hot water bottle under the sheet, here, too." Fiona pointed into the cot, smiling. "It's the nearest we can get to an incubator. Most of the time he's with his mum and that keeps him warm, but she does need some rest too, and this way he stays cosy on his own." Fiona walked with the baby into the next door room where the scales were, putting him gently down beside them and removing his clothing. "Let's see how you're doing , heh?"

The cold metal caused the baby to cry out and kick his skinny little legs in protest. Fiona frowned as she noted the weight. She dressed him again, then returned to talk with his mother. Imogen could not follow the conversation, which was in Twi but she could see the worry in both women's faces. Fiona turned toward her and explained. "It seems he's not quite strong enough to suckle properly, so we'll have to feed him through a tube. I was just discussing it with his mother. She'll have to express her milk and then we'll give it through the tube."

Imogen turned away and swallowed hard while the tube was inserted through the baby's nose and into his stomach. The very idea made her retch. Once it was safely in place Fiona took a small cup to his mother, then fed the expressed milk to the baby with a syringe. His dark eyes opened wide in his tiny wizened face as the milk hit his stomach.

"How often will he need to be fed?" Imogen asked, reaching a finger out to the baby's hand. His long thin fingers curled around her own with surprising strength. He would not let go and Fiona laughed at the expression on Imogen's face.

"Every two hours or so, to begin with. Once he gets a bit bigger he'll be able to feed himself, won't you? As you can see he's really quite a tough little chap." She settled him back with his mother on the bed. "The little babies do quite well as long as they're not premature. We can't help them much then, without an oxygen supply for them."

"What's the smallest baby you've delivered?"

"There was a set of twins that were very small. One died but the surviving one was well under a kilo when she was born. She stayed with us for six weeks." They were sitting at the table and Fiona was rolling cotton wool balls as she talked, an item used in virtually every aspect of the clinical work as far as Imogen could tell. She pushed the large roll of cotton wool towards Imogen. "Here, make yourself useful." Imogen copied her, tearing off a small amount of cotton wool and rolling it around between her palms to form a ball. The pile of completed balls grew as they chatted on.

"It's unusual for a mother to be able to stay that long. They have to get back to their families and farming."

"Yes. I noticed you have a very quick turnover," Imogen said. "What about the biggest baby, how much did that weigh?"

"Almost four and a half kilos." Fiona laughed. "They were both here at the same time. I called them Little and Large, not that anyone here understood the joke."

"Do you get any abnormal babies?"

Fiona sobered. "We've had a few. The commonest deformity is an extra digit, although I'd never seen them back home."

"What do you do with them?"

"Usually it's just soft tissue and you can ligate it and the extra bit comes off easily enough. If there's a bone in the extra finger then we just leave it."

"Ugh. I couldn't do that, even the thought gives me the colly-wobbles." Imogen shuddered. "I suppose you've got a store of horror stories you could tell me?"

"I could, if you want," Fiona's manner remained professional, although she seemed to be more relaxed about Imogen's presence now. "But seriously, the babies which are more severely or obviously deformed don't usually survive for long. The mother's reject them as soon as they see them."

"But that's terrible." Imogen flared up as quickly as ever. "How can they just abandon a new baby like that?"

Fiona shrugged. "It's a whole different prospect here, you see. Not long after I arrived we had a baby with Down's syndrome. I wanted to tell the mother right away, as we would back home, but Agnes stopped me. She said the baby wasn't that severe and if we said nothing the mother might not notice for a few weeks. If we told her right away she'd be sure to reject the baby."

"But there's such a lot can be done for Down's syndrome. How could you not tell her?" Imogen still looked stricken.

"It was hard, but Agnes was right, of course." Fiona continued. "You have to see it from their perspective. An extra burden on the family like that can be very hard here. It's alright if someone can work and pull their weight economically, but otherwise . . . It's not really a matter of choice, it's about necessity. A child with a severe disability can be a disaster. You can't really compare things with home."

"It's not fair, Fiona, it's just not fair." Imogen shook her head,

"It all seems so straightforward when you're sitting at home reading the bumf from some organisation or other. And then, when you come here and try and do something practical it all gets blurred and complicated." She was quiet for a while.

But when a woman in labour arrived both of them turned their attention to the job in hand. Fiona knew the woman, Akosua, from her initial check up at the antenatal clinic, although she hadn't been for a while. This was her fifth pregnancy. Fiona chatted to her about her family as she settled Akosua into the labour room and examined her.

Even for a full term pregnancy, Akosua's bulging abdomen was large. Imogen watched as Fiona pressed and prodded then bent her ear to listen for the baby's heartbeat with the black, trumpet-like midwife's stethoscope. Fiona raised her head and took Akosua's hand. "Akosua, I think you may have two babies in there, not just one. I'm pretty sure I can hear two heartbeats, and there are an awful lot of arms and legs."

The woman regarded her with a serious face as the words sank in. "Oh Sister, not twins?"

"I think so," Fiona nodded. It was not always welcome news so she watched Akosua's reaction carefully. She broke into an uncertain smile after a moment and Fiona relaxed. The woman was well on in labour and there was not much time for more chatter as the contractions came fast and furious. Imogen stayed to the side, as Fiona and Felicia made ready for the delivery, but not so distant as to get in the way of her growing excitement.

Within three quarters of an hour two healthy baby girls had arrived in the world. Even though she had not assisted in any way Imogen felt an enormous pride in the twins and in Fiona, who yet again impressed her with the deceptive speed of her movements. She moved over to watch the babies' first bath.

"They're a good size, these two," said Fiona as she lifted the second twin into the water. The first was safely wrapped and lying in the cot. "Both nearly three kilos. That's very good for twins."

"Her head's a funny shape, flattened on one side. They're alright, aren't they?" Imogen wanted her twins to be perfect.

"Don't worry, they're fine," Fiona reassured. "See, it's just where they've been a bit squashed together in the womb." She put the two babies close together in the cot.

"Oh. Aren't they adorable?" The two heads fitted perfectly to each other like two halves of a nut. Imogen felt as proud as if she was indeed their mother. She turned and hugged Fiona, kissing her on the cheek. "They're just like two conkers, don't you think? You know the ones with a flat side and a round side. We used to make doll's house furniture out of them with pins and wool." She beamed at Fiona hugging her again. "Two little chestnut babies. How did that happen?"

Fiona took a towel-wrapped twin back to the bench, disentangling herself from Imogen in the process. "Well, they were both born head first, so they must have been jammed down into their mother's pelvis for a while. Baby's skulls are very soft. They'll soon fill out again. They'll probably get an extra massage or two to help."

Imogen looked puzzled for a moment and then smiled. "Oh yes. I remember, you told me people massage babies' heads to be sure they grow into the right shape." Enjoying the new babies, she reached down to stroke the twin lying in the cot, but Fiona bustled about and soon had the twins tucked up with their mother.

"We better go and get some lunch before Esther burns it beyond salvation," Fiona said briskly and with a few parting words to Felicia, led the way over to the house.

26

Imogen chattered happily all through the meal. It wasn't until they were sitting in armchairs with a cup of tea that she noticed how quiet Fiona was. Not just quiet, but brooding, Imogen realised. "What is it, Fiona? What's up?"

Fiona took a careful breath before speaking, but her voice still shook. "Just what the hell did you think you were doing kissing me in front of everyone?"

Imogen was shocked by her tone, "What do you mean, when? I didn't . . . did I?"

"Right in the middle of the ward. You were all over me." Fiona's face was stormy.

"I . . . I'm sorry. I was just so excited. I didn't mean anything by it." Imogen was flabbergasted by the intensity of Fiona's attack. "I only gave you a quick hug. It wasn't anything anyone would have noticed. Women here hug each other. What's your problem?"

"Yes, but they don't see us hugging and kissing all the time, do they? I told you clearly enough about being careful here in Osubuso, didn't you understand what I said at all?"

"Oh yes," Imogen was now equally angry. "I understand alright. You've been making it perfectly clear since we got back that I'm nothing but a nuisance. But this is too much. You're so bloody terrified of what people might think, you can't even accept a friendly hug. What's the proper distance I should keep then? One yard, two? Or would you prefer a few thousand miles? Don't worry, I'll be gone soon enough and then no-one will suspect you of having any emotions at all." She stood up and moved towards her room. "I can start packing now, as my presence is so upsetting to you."

"Imogen, no." Fiona jumped up and ran after her, but Imogen shook her off and walked into her bedroom. Fiona followed, catching her by the shoulder and turning her. Imogen kept her eyes to the floor. "Imogen, please, I didn't mean ..." Fiona sat down on the edge of the bed. "Oh dammit, I'm sorry, I just get so ..." She looked up at Imogen who did not move. "Look at me, Imogen, please?"

Imogen turned her head away but spoke more quietly. "What do you want me to do, Fiona? I've hardly touched you since we got back. I've tried to do what you ask, but it seems it's not enough. I was so happy in the ward, I didn't think. It was just an innocent kiss on the cheek, for god's sake." Her voice broke slightly. "The way the twins fitted together made me think of us," she finished in a whisper.

Fiona sighed deeply and reached forward to pull Imogen against her, hiding her face against Imogen's stomach. Her voice was muffled. "I know, I know. I don't know what's the matter with me. I just get paranoid about it. I'm sorry." She pulled away slightly and looked up at Imogen. "I don't want you to go away at all, but my work is important to me and I keep thinking 'what if people suspected?' I can't jeopardise everything here just because I want a bit of sex, can I?"

"Oh, Fiona." Imogen reproached her in a voice full of tears. "Do you have to be so brutal?"

Fiona pulled Imogen down to sit on her lap, holding her face between her hands, her thumbs brushing away the tears. "I'm a clumsy bastard, aren't I? I didn't mean that how it sounded, but I'm serious, Imogen. I don't have a clue what the Ghanaians think about homosexuality. It's not exactly easy to ask about either. Even with Rebecca who's a good friend, I haven't actually discussed the issue, although she clearly understands and never acts as if it matters two hoots, but she's spent time in the UK, and I'm sure she and David have talked about all sorts of cross-cultural things like that, so I can't judge anyone else by that example. I can't afford to take the risk, there's far more important things at stake here than just our love life. Please try and understand." Fiona softened her words by brushing Imogen's hand against her lips.

"I do try, Fiona, I really do, and I do understand. It's just very hard to be kept so completely at a distance." Imogen finally turned her head to look directly at Fiona, her eyes brimming with tears.

"I know, I'm sorry, but even without this, I'd probably be just as wrapped up in work." Fiona confessed. "And I think I'm frightened that if I touch you in the privacy of the house then I'll forget outside and give us away. It could wreck the whole project if people reacted badly. I know it's not fair, it's like denying who I am, what we are, but ..." she hesitated. "I haven't really hurt you so badly that you want to go home early, have I?"

"No." Imogen admitted quietly. "I really like it here. The whole project's fascinating. I find the clinical stuff a bit scary on the whole, but this morning I found it really moving. I've only seen two births before, with Agnes or Comfort Atta. I know you've seen hundreds, but it's still so new and wonderful to me. And being there with you, and then it was twins too, two beautiful baby girls. I was just thrilled to be a part of it, and I'm still feeling very emotional, so I probably over-reacted too, I'm sorry. Pax?" She held out her little finger, linking it with Fiona's to seal the truce, then stood up. "Come on, you're right, we've got work to do and we better get back to it before anyone comes looking for us. I'll just wash my face and I'll be right as rain."

27

The morning of October twenty third arrived too quickly. Imogen's flight was at midday the next day, so Fiona suggested they go down to Accra and stay the night there. "It'll save any panics with vehicle break-downs or burst tyres and things like that."

"It would be nice to be together for our last night," Imogen agreed, "and without Esther or anyone to worry about, too." They'd only spent one night together since returning from Cape Coast, and that was accidental, resulting in a furtive early morning scamble when they heard Esther in the kitchen.

"I thought we could stay with Rebecca and David. Their place is convenient for the airport." Fiona made the suggestion tentatively. Imogen looked doubtful, so she added, "I haven't seen them for ages, and it would be nice for you to meet them."

"I was rather hoping to have you to myself." Imogen replied.

"You still would, almost. We'll go out for dinner. It would just be a bed to sleep in, really, but I'm happy to book a hotel if you'd rather." She tried to sound convincing.

"No, it's OK. If that's what you want. It would be nice to meet your friends, you're right."

By the time all the farewells were said to the project staff Imogen was quite drained. Even in such a short time she felt real friendship towards these people who had welcomed her so wholly into their lives and work. The four senior staff each brought a small parting gift, a strip of brightly coloured kente cloth from each of the Kofis and a piece of printed material from Comfort Atta in a design Imogen had admired in the market one day. But it was Agnes' gift which brought the tears to overflowing. "I made you this for the journey, Imogen, I know you like it and it travels well." She held out a small brown paper

119

package, tied with string. Inside were several large pieces of the homemade peanut brittle that Imogen had devoured at every opportunity during her stay.

"Oh Agnes. You shouldn't have." Imogen looked at each of them in turn. "None of you should have, it's too much. Thank you."

"Think of it as advance payment for the book." Kofi Paul lightened the atmosphere with a joke, and eventually everything was stowed in the car. With a final wave Imogen left the Osubuso project compound, looking backwards out of the window to keep everyone in sight as long as possible.

"God help me when I have to leave next year," Fiona said quietly from behind the wheel. "I'm upset enough just watching them say goodbye to you." She reached down, twining her fingers through Imogen's and they drove on in silence.

"What will you do when you come back home?" Imogen inquired after a while.

"I'm not sure really." Fiona glanced over at her. "I'm sort of planning to take some time out and think things over. I need to get some perspective on everything that's happened to me while I've been here, and work out what I want to do next."

"Where will you be coming back to?" asked Imogen, realising she had no idea where Fiona lived in the UK.

"Just outside of Whitby," replied Fiona with a smile. "I've got a little cottage there. It's rented out at the moment but the tenant will move out at the beginning of April and I get back in May."

Imogen gave a sigh of relief. "I suppose that's not really so far away from me, is it? At least it's in the same half of the country. I was worried you were going to say Exeter or somewhere."

"I suppose it's about three hours from Manchester," Fiona agreed, both pleased and concerned at this casual assumption that they would be meeting again. "I love being near the sea and the moors, and Whitby's a lovely old-fashioned little place but still alternative as well. It really suits me."

"I lived in Todmorden for a while," said Imogen. "It was nice to be so near to the countryside, but in the end I couldn't stand being so far from everything else. And it was a bit inward focused, I felt."

"Full of arty-farty types. I'd have thought that was right up your street, and lots of very right-on, politically correct women to mix with." Fiona teased.

"I've found plenty of them in Chorlton, actually, and it's much better for nightlife." Imogen replied lightly. "Tell me a bit more about Rebecca and David, seeing as I'm going to meet them. What do they do?"

"David's the marketing manager of a firm which produces chickens. He's worked out here for years. Rebecca trained as a teacher but she's been at home with the kids for the last few years. They're expecting their third next month. They're a lovely couple and the two boys are delightful. I'm sure you'll like them."

Imogen's mind drifted off as she imagined a happy reunion in Manchester or Whitby.

Rebecca, heavily pregnant, and the boys welcomed them at the gate. The older boy took Imogen's hand, leading her away into the back of the house. "My name's Terry. Come and see my room," he said in a solemn voice. "You'll be sleeping with Auntie Fi in here, and I'm going to sleep with Jack." He looked up at her with a touchingly serious expression. "I don't mind, you know, I always get to stay up late when there's visitors, and he doesn't snore."

"Well, it's very kind of you, anyway," said Imogen, charmed by Terry's earnest manner. She looked about the room into which he showed her. "My goodness, those are lovely paintings. Who did them?"

"I did, and Jack did those ones there," said Terry proudly. "I've got lots more." He cocked his head to one side. "You can see them if you like."

"I'd love to." Imogen studied his pictures, impressed by the detail. She noticed the younger boy standing shyly by the door. "Auntie Fi says you do drawing," he said. "I like drawing, too."

"Would you like to do some with me?" At Jack's eager nod, Imogen looked around, picking up a pencil and paper. "I tell you what, Jack, why don't you and Terry draw some squiggly lines on this paper and then we'll see how we can turn them into something else. Have you ever watched how squiggles can turn into flowers or monsters before?" The boys shook their heads, eyes wide. "Let's have a go then, look." Imogen drew a couple of wavy, curling lines. "Now you add some more." Each boy took a turn with the pencil, then Imogen held them spellbound as she transformed their scribbles into weird and wonderful cartoons with a few additional lines or some skilful shading. Several sheets of paper were covered by the time Rebecca and Fiona came to find what had happened to her.

"I'm sorry to let them monopolise you like this," said Rebecca with an apologetic smile. "We got carried away in baby talk, and I didn't notice. It was the quiet which alerted me, that usually means trouble."

"Look, Mummy. Look what Auntie Im'gen's did. They're monsters from space, and some an'mals, and these ones are pretty flowers." Jack held out several sheets for inspection, while Terry explained further, pointing. "See, we did these lines and then Auntie Imogen added those bits. She's very clever, isn't she?"

"Very clever, yes." Rebecca admired the pictures, giving Imogen a wink over the boys heads. "Come along, you two. Let's leave Auntie Fi and Imogen to get their bags unpacked. You can see them again in a little while." Rebecca urged the boys out of the room ahead of her.

Fiona set the overnight bag down on the end of the bed. A second bed had been pushed up against Terry's to form a temporary double. "The boys have really taken to you. They're very sweet, don't you think?"

Imogen nodded, "Yes, they seem a nice pair. Terry's quite talented with a pencil. Did you catch up with all Rebecca's news?"

"Mmmm, oh yes. Everything's going fine." Fiona looked at her watch. "I was thinking we could go out to the Tebora Beach Hotel to eat tonight. It's a bit quieter than the restaurants in town. Unless you had something particular in mind?"

"No. That sounds fine. What time do we need to go?"

"About eight? I usually do the boys' bedtime story when I'm here."

"So there's no rush then." Imogen raised her hands to Fiona's neck and removed the barrette imprisoning her hair. She spread the rich chestnut length around Fiona's shoulders and twined her fingers into it. "That's better," she murmured softly, lowering her mouth to Fiona's, and finding a warm welcome.

Despite its high quality, Fiona hardly tasted the food. She watched as Imogen ate heartily, unable to match her happy unconcern. After the meal they went to sit in the hotel garden, overlooking the beach.

"It reminds me of Cape Coast here, although the atmosphere's a lot more managed, not so natural." Imogen said quietly, setting her beer back on the table. She dropped her hand to take Fiona's in the shadow between their seats. "We had a lovely time there, didn't we?"

In response Fiona reached into the woven bag that she always carried and drew out a lumpy package. She put this before Imogen on the table. "Go on, open it."

Imogen lifted the package, testing its weight and shape before she undid the wrapping paper. Inside was a mug from the Winneba pottery shop they'd visited. It was dark blue with a bird-like figure in charcoal grey on one side, and an abstract symbol on the other. She turned it in her hands, examining the glaze, "Fiona, it's beautiful. When did you get it? And what do these mean?"

"This one is an adinkra symbol, called 'sankofa', and this," Fiona pointed to the figure of the bird, "well, it's another version of the same proverb. See, it has its head reaching back plucking its own tail feathers but it's moving forward at the same time."

"Oh yes, I see. But what does 'sankofa' represent, then?"

"It's about taking what's useful from the past with us into the future rather than just abandoning everything because it's old."

"A sort of Ghanaian forget-me-not?" Imogen was delighted with her gift. She looked around, "It's a shame there's so many people here, or I'd thank you properly," she grinned. The grin widened as she saw the blush rise in Fiona's cheek and she leaned forward suggestively.

"Behave yourself." Fiona said.

"I'll think of you every time I have a cup of coffee," said Imogen, "not that I need this lovely mug to make me think of you." Their eyes met and there was a short silence. "You won't forget me altogether, will you?"

"No," Fiona said, feeling increasingly unsettled by Imogen's easy assumption of a shared future.

As ever, Imogen took the direct route. "You do want to see me when you come home, don't you? I mean, I want this to be more than a tropical idyll."

Fiona met her searching gaze only briefly before her eyes returned to the less unnerving view of the sea. She spoke slowly, weighing her words. "I don't know, Imogen. It has been a lovely idyll, something special. I've really enjoyed this time with you. I'm not denying the attraction, how could I? But even in just two weeks we've had arguments. I just don't feel sure enough to make us both hostage to a future that may not be realistic." She was acutely aware of Imogen's disappointment. The silence hung between them for almost a minute.

"I know we've only been lovers for a little while, but I feel we've got to know each other in other ways too, all those evenings talking over Scrabble. There's more to my feelings for you than simple sexual attraction, you know. I think there's a foundation to build on, if you'd just give it a try."

"Maybe I just see the fragility of that foundation more easily than it's strength. Six months is long enough for anything to happen. You'll be back among your familiar friends and mixing with all sorts of interesting and attractive women. You shouldn't restrict your options for my sake."

"Don't go blaming me in advance for something I haven't done, and give me some credit for understanding my own feelings." She kept her voice low but the hurt and anger carried clearly. "After all, I'm not the one who's backtracking, desperate to avoid any sort of commitment. Look, if you want to end it now, that's fine, but just tell me straight that you don't want me. I can take an honest rejection, just so long as that's really what you want."

And Fiona opened her mouth to take advantage of this easy way out of her dilemma, only to be ambushed by her deeper feelings. "If I said I didn't want you it wouldn't be honest at all, and if nothing else, you're right, you deserve honesty." She paused. "I do want you, and if I'm honest, then I think I'm afraid. Afraid of making the commitment and then not being able to see it through, of letting you down when I get too wrapped up in some new project, and I will. That's how I am. I've tried to warn you, I'm only likely to hurt you more if I make promises it turns out I can't keep." Finally Fiona's eyes met Imogen's and the look held.

Imogen reached out and joined their hands again. "I don't want you to promise anything you're not sure of. I really only want one small promise, that we don't give up now, before we've really gone anywhere with this whole experiment. Yes, anything can happen in six months, but that's true between us as well. We can decide to kill off whatever feelings we have, right now, or we can decide to give them a chance and see what develops. I really want that chance. It's not too much to ask, is it?"

Fiona shook her head. "Not when you put it like that, no. I think I'd like that chance too, but I'm not sure I'm brave enough to take it."

"We'll take it together, then. No promises. No pressure. And if what we feel for each other grows and we put down roots together, wonderful. But if the feelings shrivel and die away for lack of nourishment, we'll say so as gently as we can. Does that sound fair?"

"I think I can live with that, so long as you can tell me what I've done to deserve such a caring and careful woman in my life," Fiona said with a tender smile.

"Well, I certainly can't do that here. Let's go back and I can give you a long and thorough explanation."

Part Four: *Breaking New Ground*

29

The room echoed to the mellow jazz piano and trumpet of Abdullah Ibrahim, bringing the rhythm of the South African township into the cold dark of south Manchester in early February. Imogen swayed as she bent over the clay on her table. After a moment she stood back and surveyed her handiwork with a critical eye. Yes, it was just about ready for the glaze now. She smoothed over the clay a final time, then put it to one side.

Wiping her hands on a rag, she ran her fingers through her hair and arched back to stretch the day's crouch out of her spine. "That will have to do for tonight." She draped a protective cover over the nearly finished piece, tidied the bench and switched off the light as she left the room.

She was working on a number of pieces based on her trips to Bangladesh and Ghana. The two themes of flood and drought created an interesting contrast but she was finding it a challenge to create the dry, cracked look she wanted in the Ghanaian works. The smooth fluidity of the Bangladesh pieces was easier but she knew the glaze had to be rich enough to convey the idea of flowing water.

As she waited for the kettle to boil, she shuffled through the post which Carla had placed on the hall table. Financial necessity meant that Imogen always had a lodger. Carla had been with her since just after her return from Osubuso, and so knew all about Fiona.   Nothing of interest, she thought. *'There should be one from Fiona soon, surely'*. She anticipated each letter with a mixture of emotions, hoping it would contain something more personal than the details of life in Osubuso, but was almost always disappointed. Imogen sometimes wondered if the affair had been a figment of her imagination, there was so little evidence of it left. "Nothing but work, work, work. It wouldn't

kill her to put in something personal now and then, would it?"
she'd expostulated one morning. Carla responded with a shrug.
"I don't know why you get so wound up, Imogen. It's the same
every time."

Imogen poured her tea and wandered into the sitting room.
Carla was curled into her usual corner of the settee, eyes glued
to the TV. Imogen sat on the beanbag and waited for the soap
episode to finish. Having a lodger made her finances more
secure, there was no doubt about that, but sometimes she
thought it would be nice to have the house entirely to herself.
Not that Carla was difficult. They got on well together, sharing
both the space and domestic tasks without animosity.

Carla worked at the university in the media studies
department. The early evening was the only time they were both
in the house together as Imogen, after her solitary day, usually
spent the evenings either at meetings or socialising. Carla, who
was out all day, loved nothing better than to collapse in front of
the television at night, justifying the practice by insisting it was
necessary for her work. Friday and Saturday would find her
cruising the local nightclubs, on the look out for new attractions.
Imogen never quite knew who she would find joining them for
a weekend breakfast.

The familiar theme music came on and Carla looked over at
Imogen. "So who is it tonight, then, Womankind Worldwide,
Amnesty, Friends of the Earth? I can never keep up with all this
second Tuesday, and third Monday of the month stuff." She
grinned at Imogen, shaking her head.

"It's the Amnesty letter writing group tonight," Imogen
responded good naturedly. "We're meeting in the Red Lion at eight,
so I better get going. I just wanted to tell you I'm going to Safeway
tomorrow, so add anything you want to the list in the kitchen."

"OK, thanks. I thought we could do with a few dishcloths, and
I really liked that bread you got last time, too." Carla's attention
turned back to the screen as the next soap tune swelled up
louder. "Have a good scribble then. 'Night."

Imogen was putting away the shopping the following
afternoon when the phone rang. "Hello."

"I'd like to speak to Imogen Pollock, please." It was a male
voice.

"Yes, speaking. Who's calling?"

"My name is James Hughes, from Square Space Galleries. I'm ringing about the portfolio you submitted to us a couple of months ago."

Imogen's heart leapt into her mouth. On her return from Osubuso she'd spotted the request for bids from artists wishing to exhibit in the gallery. She'd managed to put together a reasonable submission in the few days before the deadline. "Oh, yes." She tried to keep her voice non-committal, feeling it hard to breathe.

James Hughes continued, "The exhibition committee would like to talk to you about your submission. They've suggested next Wednesday at ten o'clock. Would that be a possibility for you?"

"Yes, yes, I can make that, no problem." Imogen did not pretend a need to check in her non-existent diary. "Should I come to the Galleries, or will the meeting be somewhere else?"

"Good. Yes, the meeting will be in the Galleries. If you ask for me at the reception, I can show you through when they're ready for you." He paused, then went on more confidentially, "I shouldn't really say this, but I can't resist. I thought your work was quite superb. They'll be seeing two or three others, as well, but I'm hoping you get the spot."

"Thank you, thank you very much." Imogen could have hugged him in her delight.

"Well, then. I'll see you next Wednesday. Bye till then." James Hughes was gone and the handset buzzed emptily in Imogen's hand. She stared at it in amazement before replacing it on the cradle, then as the news sank in she danced a jig of celebration. Square Space Galleries had an excellent reputation and had been the launchpad for several local artist's careers. It was in a good central location, taking up three floors of a refurbished mill building.

'*Hold on, girl, hold on. It's only like an interview. You haven't got it yet*'. She tried to calm down, but James' words of praise echoed in her head. '*Oh, shit! An exhibition of my own. Bloody hell!*' Imogen hit her hand to her forehead. '*I'll never have enough to fill a whole gallery*'. She dashed into the studio.

Imogen's studio was a long narrow room extending from the back of the house. Originally it was a kitchen but she had converted the space as soon as she moved in, altering the rear downstairs room into a kitchen-dining room at the same time. There was a window all along the room making it light and airy. Both sides were lined with benches and shelves leaving enough of a gap to walk up and down the centre. A small kiln took up most of one corner.

The studio was not the only room devoted to art in the house; there was also a darkroom upstairs which had previously been part of a large bathroom. Some of the extra space had been sacrificed, but it had been worth it, saving Imogen a small fortune in processing and developing costs.

She was in the studio for some hours becoming steadily more annoyed with herself. Nothing seemed to work. The clay would not do as she wished. She started several attempts first at one work about the drought, then another abstract piece, but each time it ended in disaster. Angrily she threw the clay back into the bin. "Damn, damn, damn!" She bit her lip in frustration. "Some bloody sculptor you are." She turned back to her sketch book, flicking through the pages. The sketches were of the twins she'd seen born. She was trying to capture the essence of their twinship, the way they were moulded to one another. "But I can see it so clearly, why can't I do it?" she muttered.

Her mind flipped back to the actual birth and she remembered Fiona's swift, sure movements, wasting no energy, doing exactly what was needed with a minimum of fuss. Imogen felt the tension go out of her shoulders as she drew a long deep breath and let it go again. *"You stupid idiot,"* she reprimanded herself. *"The exhibition's not till later this year. They only want to talk to you on Wednesday, not see the whole shebang. There's no need to rush about like a lunatic. There's plenty of time."*

Osubuso
February 14th

Dear Imogen,

Sorry not to write for an age, I keep meaning to but you know how it gets here. I'm grabbing a bit of peace and quiet while I'm on-call. There's a woman in labour and I'm waiting for Felicia to call me for the delivery. It will probably be within the hour, so I'm not bothering going to bed.

We've had the harmattan blowing for the last week or so and everything's covered in dust again. Just like when you first saw it last year. I'm glad of my cardie if I get called in the early hours as it's a bit chilly (at least by Ghanaian standards).

I saw our twins the other day at the weighing clinic. They're growing well and very beautiful. Akosua asked me how the other Sister was.

You know how you decorated the labour room for us, with all the prints around the wall? Well, I think you've started a trend. One of Kofi's youth groups came to do the outside painting for all the buildings and they've put similar borders around each one. The whole compound looks really cheerful. The outpatients has a border of silhouettes of big and little people and the ward has babies and mums with bumps. The quality of the art isn't great, but it's very cheerful to look at.

Agnes, Comfort Atta and me do the interviews for the new midwife next week. We've got two or three really good looking applications so I'm hopeful we'll get someone suitable. Keep your fingers crossed. Otherwise I'm busy trying to work out everything that has to be done in the next couple of months before I leave. I'm not sure how I feel about coming home now it's getting so close.

Oh, here's Felicia now, sorry, have to dash,

Fiona.

PS. Happy Valentine's Day!

Chorlton
March 5th

Dear Fiona,

I can't believe it. I actually got chosen for the exhibition at Square Space Galleries! I get a whole exhibition to myself, the whole of one floor. They want to show both the sculpting and the photographic stuff. I was chosen out of four people, I mean that was the shortlist, there were lots more applications, it was just four of us who were interviewed. It was really nerve-wracking. Mine was first thing in the morning so I had to hang around all day waiting while they did the others. They'd said they'd tell us that afternoon so I couldn't leave. I almost took up smoking I was so tense! My sanity was only saved by James. He's like the exhibition manager for the Galleries and he's a darling. He was so sweet, kept checking whether I wanted anything and trying to distract me with chatter. He seems to know everything and everyone. Before you get worried, not that you will I know, he's as gay as they come. I learned a few interesting snippets about people on the scene here, which I won't tell you as I know you don't go in for gossip, and anyway you don't know any of them, but you wouldn't believe what's going on. Anyway, I'm working like a madwoman to make sure I have enough good stuff to fill the space. This could be my big break. The only down side is that the exhibition's scheduled for late May/early June, just when you get back. I'm going to be up to my eyes in it but I want to spend time catching up with you too. Do you have a definite date yet? Oh and thanks for the Valentine's Day wishes. I spent the day trying to persuade the public to part with their money for a good cause, in other words I was shaking a tin for Survival in the centre of Manchester. I managed to collect about fifty quid but it's tough going these days. I heard from Nigel last week that he's seen the proofs for the book and they're OK. They'll send me a final copy in a week or two. Seems like everything's coming good all at once, doesn't it? All I need is for you to be here at home too.

Love you and miss you,

Imogen
xxxxxxx

As soon as she saw the big oblong parcel Fiona knew it was the book. She held it in her hands feeling the solid weight. '*I suppose I better open it and see how it turned out*', she thought, still worrying about how she featured in it despite reassurances from Imogen and Nigel that it was a well- balanced work. She put it back down on the table. '*Maybe I'll get the others to look at it first, I don't want to spoil their enjoyment. I can look at it after them*'.

It took a little while before the four senior staff were gathered in the house. Fiona hadn't told them anything and she could see the puzzlement on their faces. She held up the parcel. "I found this in the post box today. Can you guess what it is?"

"Is it, our book?" Comfort Atta's voice was hesitant but at Fiona's nod she broke into a wide smile. "Oh Fiona, why haven't you opened it? How could you bear to wait?"

The others made similarly excited noises. Fiona handed the parcel to Kofi Paul. "Here you are, deputy, I think you should do the honours."

Kofi Paul took the parcel and undid the wrapping slowly and methodically. Inside the book was protected by a layer of bubble-wrap but they could immediately see the dark red cover. "Ooh, it looks lovely," cooed Agnes.

Kofi Paul folded back the last of the wrappings and turned the book over so that its front cover faced toward them. The title was in bold green lettering across the top: "Survival Skills" and slightly smaller below "Daily Life in the Osubuso Project". Underneath was a square photograph of the One Woman Plenty Chop seating area, full of customers, with Osubuso market in the background, stalls covered with produce, and the people looking cheerful in their multicoloured cloths.

"It looks good, I like the colours." Kofi said approvingly.

"Well, I want you all to have a good look at it, so make yourselves comfortable." Fiona placed a cold drink in front of each Ghanaian. "I'm going to check on the clinic. I'll see it after you've finished. It's really your book." Unusually there was no dissent to her suggestion.

Down in the clinic she found Kittewaa and Comfort B seeing to the last of the people queueing for treatment. The problems were straightforward enough so she moved on. The drug store was a bit untidy with the comings and goings of a busy day. Fiona sorted through the rows of medicine, noting which ones needed reordering in the book hanging from the shelves. It was an odd feeling to think she'd only be putting in one more order to the Ministry in Afafranto before she left.

From the outpatients building she made her rounds of the maternity ward lingering to chat with the mothers and admire their babies. It was relatively quiet with only four women but that could well change, with Patience on duty for the night, she reflected, glad that her own on-call was completed that morning. She checked through the small drug stock in the labour room which was in order. Unable to find any other reason for delay she went back to the house and the waiting book.

The four Ghanaians were still sitting around her table talking, although the book was now closed. They looked up as she came through the door. Kofi Paul spoke first. "It's wonderful. It is a true portrait of life here in Osubuso. Imogen is such a good photographer."

Agnes joined in, "She catches people in such a way, I don't know, she sees everything."

"There is certainly something of everyone in here." Kofi tapped the cover of the book gently. "It's a shame that many people in Osubuso will never see it."

Fiona responded quickly. "There's no reason why they shouldn't, after all we have this copy, we can show it to whoever we like."

Comfort Atta spoke, as always with a practical point in mind. "We could let people see this one, but we would need to take great care or it will become worn out." She pursed her lips considering possibilities. "We would have to organise it well, just a certain number each day, and someone always around to see no harm is done. Kofi, do you think one of the youth groups could be put in charge?"

Kofi nodded. "It is possible. But there are so many people in Osubuso, thousands, it will take a long, long time."

"We are in no hurry." Comfort Atta's mind was clearly made up. "Fiona, could we set aside one room in the outpatients for viewing? We managed with less when the malnourished children had to stay there. I don't see a problem in losing just one room, do you?"

Fiona shook her head smiling. It was good to see Comfort Atta taking charge like this. "If you can really organise it so that everyone who wants to will see the book, then please, go ahead."

Comfort Atta stood up, followed by the other three, and they said their goodnights. Fiona moved over to the table and sat down pulling the book toward her. '*Well, I better get it over with. They all seem very pleased, so maybe I really am worrying over nothing*'.

After a few minutes she was as deeply absorbed as her Ghanaian colleagues had been. She turned the first few pages, a series of full page photographs, and was immediately enthralled. The photography was truly superb, as she knew it would be. She had intended to flip through quickly to judge the balance between the project and the local people, between the senior staff and herself, but she couldn't. Each image seemed a masterpiece. She was amazed by how much Imogen had captured of life in Osubuso. There were images Fiona could not remember seeing in her three years, yet Imogen had spotted them in only a few short weeks.

The text, too, was excellent, explaining and clarifying but never competing with the visual feast which included a few pencil sketches as well. A photograph of her at work caught her by surprise. She'd almost forgotten her reason for such a close examination. Her own image was scattered through the pages of the book but hardly ever took precedence. In the sections which focused on her work, Imogen used the text cleverly to keep the Ghanaians in the reader's mind. And the symbiotic relationship between the project and the local people, the external funds and the home-grown effort, was the book's central theme. At last Fiona let go of her anxiety and admitted it was a triumph.

Fiona closed the book and sat back in her chair. Perhaps this would be the most appreciated product of the whole Osubuso project she reflected with a twinge of jealousy, especially if the full scale viewing got under way. That would be something to tell Imogen.

32

By mid May Imogen was almost ready for the exhibition. The sculptures were completed and she was putting the finishing touches to the photographic pieces. Most of these were simple, but she'd included a couple of photo-montage and mosaic items too. These were a new departure and she was unsure of their effect.

Regarding the mosaic she was not even sure she wanted to display it publicly. It was based on the photos she had taken in the seaside cabin at Cape Coast. She had assembled these, cleverly using the shapes and shading within the small individual shots to create a striking slightly abstract portrait of Fiona. Imogen knew it was good but was hesitating over Fiona's possible reaction. She wished she could ask permission, but it was too late to write, and anyway she had to decide soon, if not today.

The phone rang and she looked at her watch. Sure enough it was James. "Have you got everything ready, pet? The van's just leaving now and will be with you in about half an hour. I thought I might come along and lend a hand?"

"Oh, would you? That would be great. I need someone to help me with a decision."

"OK. See you soon." James hung up. Imogen made her way back into the studio and checked over the boxes again. "Nine, ten, eleven, that's right." They were having a run through today, testing the placement of each piece. From now until the exhibition opened everything would be stored at Square Space. Imogen went upstairs to fetch the framed photos.

The gallery staff took care with the boxed sculptures she saw with relief. It was hard to let anyone else take such responsibility and she was glad James was there to oversee things. She trusted him. He came back in from the street. "Now, what was the decision you wanted help with? Having problems in your love life?" he teased.

"No, but I could be if I don't get this right," Imogen grinned back at him. "I want your opinion about whether a particular work fits in with the rest of the pieces or not, and whether I ought to show it at all, I suppose." She led the way upstairs.

James was all eyes, absorbing any clues about Imogen's personal life. Luckily the house was relatively tidy and Carla's door was closed. Imogen grinned again as she heard his sigh of disappointment. She led him into her own room and pointed to the portrait of Fiona which was standing against the wall. "That's the one I'm hesitating over."

James stood and scrutinised the picture for a few minutes before moving closer. He traced the lines of the face with his finger. "It's very good, I can't see why you're hesitating," he said. "I'd be sorry to leave it out. What are your concerns, before I say any more?"

"I just think it's got a different feel than the other pieces. I don't know what to put it with."

"And the more personal reason?" James lifted an inquiring eyebrow.

"I haven't asked her if she minds. I mean, I told her when I took the photos that they were for a portrait, but," Imogen stopped, still indecisive.

"Who is she?" asked James, but without the overtone of salaciousness which usually accompanied such a question from him. "And is she likely to see it?"

"Fiona. I met her in Ghana and yes, she's likely to see it. She gets home just as the exhibition opens." Imogen looked at James helplessly. "I don't want to upset her with it."

James turned back to the picture. "I can't see anything to object too," he said slowly. "I mean none of the smaller images are that revealing. She's obviously not a prude, she let you take them after all." The saucy lift of the eyebrow returned in full force.

"But what would we put it with? I still think it's a bit too different."

"I've got an idea, but I can't tell without trying it. Can we take it in now, along with all the rest? You can bring it back if you don't like it."

Imogen agreed, picking up the frame and carrying it carefully down to the waiting vehicle. She left it with James while she supervised the placement of the other items. It took some time to decide just which pieces went most effectively together. Imogen thought at first of having one room for Ghana, one for Bangladesh and one for other work but when she tried this it looked wrong. Instead she created a random mix, feeling reasonably happy with the result.

She went in search of James and a cup of tea. While she drank he went to cast his expert eye over the progress made so far. After about twenty minutes he came back into the room and pulled her to her feet. "Come and see what you think. I've made a few changes, and I've placed the portrait where I think it works."

Imogen retraced her steps through the display. The layout of the square interconnecting rooms gave the gallery its name. A stairway led into one corner of the large main room from which three openings led into the others. It was possible to walk through the rooms in sequence or go in and out of each directly from the main room. The room to the right of the stairwell was significantly smaller than the others. James had altered the positioning of several pieces to good effect. Now each of the three larger rooms had a focal item at its centre, nicely balanced by the remaining pieces around it.

Reaching the third room, Imogen turned to James, a question rising to her lips. "I thought you said you'd put it in somewhere."

In answer James pointed her into the fourth room. Imogen walked through the doorway and stopped. The portrait filled the left hand wall, softly lit from a window high on the right. There was nothing to distract from it. It was as if the small space had been specially created as a mini gallery for just such a purpose. She turned to James. "It's absolutely splendid. It finishes the whole thing off perfectly. You're a genius." She hugged him tightly, placing a smacking kiss soundly on his lips.

"I think it's pretty good. Thanks for the compliment." He wiped the back of his hand over his mouth in mock horror. "I think the rest of the work is better a bit less spread out, too. You're sure the mysterious Fiona won't mind?"

"I can't take it out now I've seen it here. She'll have to like it."

33

Fiona lay in her bed listening to the sounds of the wakening compound outside. Someone, probably Esther, was sweeping, the regular swish and rustle of the reed broom a soothing murmur. Further off she heard the thump of the pounding stick as women prepared the day's food. There was the occasional lilt of a voice, mothers calling or children playing together. Even at this early hour someone had a cassette player going and a reggae beat floated in from the town.

The weight of the day's events pressed Fiona into her bed making her limbs leaden, constricting her chest. She felt totally unprepared for this moment now it had finally arrived. Her last morning in Osubuso. Her eyes roved the room searching for the familiar signs of her occupancy but these were erased. Instead there were two suitcases, one worn and tattered, the other brand new, standing forlorn against the far wall, and a motley collection of cardboard boxes. Fiona closed her eyes. The ordeal of gift giving the previous day had left her drained, although the pleasure of her four friends was some compensation. Now there were just a couple of things left to do and she would be gone.

There was a tap on the door and Esther entered with her tea. "Good morning, Sister." Esther's eyes too travelled the walls noting the bare patches, the empty shelves. She did not quite meet Fiona's gaze as she put the mug on the wooden case which served as a temporary bedside cabinet.

"Thanks, Esther." Fiona managed a smile. "It doesn't really feel such a good morning to me, today. I won't have anyone to look after me back at home the way you do, will I?" She sat up and reached for the drink.

With Esther's interruption Fiona's mood changed into a spurt of rapid action. She jumped from the bed, washed quickly and was soon dressed and, on the surface, ready to face the day. She picked up a package from on top of a suitcase and went through to the sitting room. Esther was busy in the kitchen, and hearing her, called. "It's nearly ready, Sister. I'm coming." Fiona waited obediently at the table.

Esther placed toast and two poached eggs before her, the smell catching at the back of Fiona's throat. Fiona stopped her as she turned back to the kitchen. "Esther, just a minute. This is for you."

"For me? But Sister," Esther's face was a picture, her expression changing through surprise to delight and then to sadness as she took the soft, bulky parcel from Fiona's outstretched hand.

"It's just a little something. An appreciation for how you've looked after me so well."

"Oh, Sister Fiona." Tears sprang to Esther's eyes as she undid the wrapping paper and lifted out the contents. Inside was a full traditional outfit in a navy and white adinkra print, complete with an extra headcloth. Esther held it up against her body.

"I hope it fits you. I checked with Felicia before I gave it to the seamstress." Fiona's breakfast lay neglected, the eggs congealing on her plate.

"Me da wo ase, me da wo ase paa." The familiar Twi phrases were spoken in a whisper. Then breaking the habit of three years Esther moved to hug Fiona where she sat at the table. "It's beautiful, Sister. Thank you." Suddenly recovering herself Esther stood up, passing a hand over her face. "You better eat your breakfast before it gets too cold," she scolded and retreated to the kitchen still clutching her gift.

Fiona dutifully cut into her toast and egg but it was a struggle to swallow over the lump in her own throat. In the end she ate the egg but left the toast, knowing that for once Esther would not be offended. '*Just how am I going to get through today in one piece*', she wondered dolefully.

In an attempt to find comfort in following familiar routines Fiona went over to the maternity ward and spent an hour with the mothers and babies. This was only a partial success as the women were also aware of her imminent departure. One of them with three children already and now newborn twin boys, joked "Sister, I will give you this one to take home with you, then you will always have Ghana in your life."

Fiona smiled and shook her head. "Thank you, but I think you would miss him too much." She handed the sleeping infant back to his mother and wandered aimlessly back to the house.

David was coming to pick her up between one and two. On arriving in Accra, they were to collect Rebecca, Terry, Jack and six month old Fifi from the house, and then all go on to the airport. Her flight was at nine thirty that night. It was only ten thirty in the morning. She wished desperately that she was already on the plane, safely anonymous among the other passengers and able to bury her emotions for a while. Ignoring Esther's pretence of a scowl she made herself a cup of coffee and sat on the back verandah willing the time to pass.

It wasn't simply parting from such special friends as the Osubuso staff had become that was weighing her down. There were also decisions to be made about her future. She had a meeting at ActionFirst's Birmingham office the day after her arrival back in the UK. Nigel wanted to discuss the possibility of a different role within the organisation. He hadn't given her many details. All she knew was that it was related to the planned expansion of ActionFirst's programme in sub-Saharan Africa. And then there was Imogen. Over the past few months, Fiona had built up a picture of Imogen's hectic work and social life, full of events and people to whom she herself felt no real connection. The upcoming exhibition, due to open the day of Fiona's return to the UK, was clearly a momentous event. Now, more than ever, Fiona found it impossible to envisage a joint future. It would surely be best to let the affair fade gently away.

A commotion at the front of the house roused her and before she could move to investigate, Kofi Paul and Agnes came through the back door. "Sister Fiona, could you come a minute, there is something we need you for." Agnes's voice was urgent and Fiona rose immediately.

"What is it? What's happened?" She followed them to the front of the house and was through the door before she registered the crowd gathered outside. As she stopped in bewilderment they all burst into song. Fiona stared, her mouth gaping, as she let her eyes take in the people before her. All the project staff were present but there were many others too, women from the co-operatives, some of the youth group members, the mothers from the ward and one or two of the market mamas. The sound they produced made her spine tingle and she felt the tears overflow again onto her cheeks.

The song ended and Kofi Paul stepped out from behind her. He swept an arm round to include the whole crowd in the words he spoke. "Sister Fiona, this is how most of us think and speak of you. At first it was because you were working in the clinic and like all nurses, we gave you the title, 'Sister'. But within only a short time this name took another meaning and now we use it to mean our sister, part of our family." He paused and looked around. "For some of us you are an elder sister, for some, younger, but for all of us you are very dear. We cannot find the words to express this, the song we sang is one of farewell. We are sad to see you leave, but happy that we have known you."

Fiona was utterly overwhelmed, not so much by Kofi Paul's words, wonderful as these were, but by the depth of the love she could feel coming from the people around her. She could only stand helplessly in front of them. She felt a touch at her side and Comfort Atta pushed a handkerchief into her hand, placing her arm around Fiona's back. Looking up Fiona saw tears in her eyes too. They gave each other watery smiles and Fiona gripped Comfort Atta to her. Kofi Paul was still talking.

"We know you will not forget us, that you will take us with you in your heart just as we keep you here, but even so we have something for you to take away with you." One of the market mamas stepped forward holding a carrier bag. Fiona thought of how many times she had bought groundnuts from this woman. "We have chosen this design to show you will always belong in Osubuso. It belongs to our queen mother." The woman drew out a cloth from the bag and, with the help of many willing hands, spread it wide to its full six by six foot size.

It was a magnificent piece of kente, rich in orange, blue and green with a design more intricate than Fiona had seen before. She picked up an edge in her fingers. The weaving was smooth as silk. She opened and shut her mouth several times before managing to produce any sound. "Me da wo ase. Thank you." She looked around the crowd of faces, "those are very small words for what I feel, but I can only repeat it. I don't know what else to say. Thank you." Fiona reached out to embrace each of her friends in turn.

Gradually the crowd drifted away, each one with a special word for her, until only Kofi Paul, Agnes, Kofi, Comfort Atta and Margaret, the new midwife were left. Fiona was dry-eyed now, exhausted by the heightened emotions. Agnes folded the splendid cloth carefully back into it's bag. "I hope you have just a little space left in your suitcase," she joked.

"Food is ready, Sister." Esther's gentle voice brought Fiona's attention back to the room and she looked up. "Sister Agnes sent Kittewaa and Felicia to help me," Esther explained, forestalling her.

The table was set for six and in the middle were two large dishes each filled with one of Fiona's favourite Ghanaian foods, one was red-red, the mixture of beans and kelewele, and the other was groundnut stew; each had a label in the shape of a cat. She laughed, suddenly releasing them all from the melancholy of the morning. The meal turned into a celebration as each of them vied to remember the most outrageous story from the events of the previous three years.

Then, all too quickly, David arrived, Fiona's luggage was stowed in his car and her final goodbyes came due. Her last remark was for Kittewaa, "Don't forget to take Nkatia and Kelewele home with you tonight." And then she was in the car, moving down the road, staring rigidly ahead and feeling as if she was being torn in two. David was sensitive enough to remain quiet for most of the journey.

Part Five: *Uncertain Summer.*

34

Fiona forced her mind to focus in ActionFirst's modest conference room, while her brain was stranded somewhere over the Sahara. Spending the previous twenty four hours in a nondescript Birmingham hotel had not helped but, the timing of the meeting made it pointless to attempt to get home to Whitby first.

Nigel and Keith both appeared oblivious to her peculiar emotional state, however. The men were determined to extract the maximum information from her during the debriefing. The format they followed dealt with every aspect of her three year assignment in depth, from recalling her early impressions and frustrations, through to assessing where and how the support from the UK office could have been more effective and what difficulties she foresaw for the Osubuso project in the coming year. Putting her internal upheaval to one side, Fiona found this serious analysis of her work and the processes of development absorbing.

They continued well into the afternoon by which time Fiona was very tired. Eventually Nigel brought the proceedings to an end. "Well, I think that covers everything, Fiona, my dear. It only remains to thank you for all your efforts on ActionFirst's behalf out there in Osubuso. I think we can be confident that you have left the project in a strong position to continue, and the more critical points you've raised in relation to the role of this office will be acted upon, you may be sure of that." Nigel leant back in his chair and ran his hands through his thinning hair. "I think we could all do with a break, now, but, if you're not entirely worn out, my dear, I would like to spend some time discussing your possible role in the future of our work in Africa. Maybe if you came up to my office in about half, three quarters of an hour, would that be OK? It seems to make sense to deal with everything now rather than dragging you back from the wilds of Yorkshire in just a few days time. I'm sure you'll want to stay put for a while once you actually get home." Nigel was apologetic, finally remembering that Fiona was only halfway through her journey.

Taking the opportunity to grab some fresh air, Fiona went out for a quick walk. She came back to the office unexpectedly chilled having forgotten that even at this time of year, the northern sun held little power. She grabbed a hot cup of tea before making her way up to Nigel's office. Despite her tiredness she was eager to hear more about the position on offer.

Her interest grew as Nigel explained in full the role he had in mind for her. "As you already know, we're planning a significant expansion to the programme in sub-Saharan Africa. There are several reasons why this is happening now. There's obviously the increased focus on development work as a positive strategy to reduce the influence of fundamentalist groups coming from politicians on both right and left. We will be able to capitalise on that to some extent. But more importantly, there is a new coherence among many of the UK-based development agencies with a commitment to much more coordinated working practices. We're on the verge of finalising partnership agreements with at least two of the major players. ActionFirst will benefit from the increased fundraising capacity and they will benefit from our acknowledged expertise in innovative project design and management." Nigel smiled at her across his desk before continuing. "And that's where you come in, my dear. If we are to maintain our side of this new partnership we need personnel with the ability to deliver."

Fiona responded, "I can see that it will mean a significant expansion for ActionFirst, yes, but exactly what sort of work is it going to be?" She couldn't see herself in a role that involved the sort of high profile PR work that would be needed to keep these new partnerships sweet. That wasn't what she wanted at all.

"Well, my hope is to have ActionFirst programmes firmly established in an additional ten countries over the next five years. That means a lot of work on identifying potential partners in those countries, making the essential contacts to attract good local staff, and a tremendous amount of support as the new programmes develop. Osubuso is an excellent example of the sort of project we'd like to establish, and we know that it's success is attributable in no small extent to the leadership you've shown over the past three years. I'd like that example to be replicated across the new programmes. Your role would be to foster those new programmes, steering them in the right direction during the vital early years."

Fiona was immediately cautious. "But the context in each country will be entirely different. We can't just replicate Osubuso lock, stock and barrel, that's never going to work. We'd have to find the right structure, develop the appropriate mechanisms in each place."

Nigel beamed at her. "It's precisely that quality in you that makes you so suited to the role, my dear Fiona. You have a talent for identifying those very characteristics, for knowing what can be built upon and what needs to be adapted or replaced. When I say I want to replicate Osubuso, I mean replicate its success and the way it's so firmly grounded in the local situation. I believe you could make a tremendous impact if you took up the challenge of this expanded role."

"It would certainly be a challenge," Fiona agreed. Then suddenly she gave a huge yawn. "Sorry, Nigel, I'm whacked. I don't think I can last much longer. Do you need a decision right now?"

"No, no, of course not." Nigel shook his head vigorously. "You need to take your time with any decision. Besides the details aren't finalised yet, job description, salary, benefits, all that stuff. All I need now is confirmation that you would be interested." At Fiona's confirmatory nod, he continued, "Good. I'll make sure you get the full details just as soon as we've agreed them, and we can start the formal selection process. I can't think of anyone with a stronger claim to this position than you, my dear, although obviously it can't be guaranteed."

Fiona nodded again, trying unsuccessfully to suppress another yawn as Nigel finally let her go. Luckily the hotel was nearby. The combination of the tiring debriefing and the lack of sleep from her overnight flight finally hit her like a sledgehammer. Fiona fell into the bed and a dreamless sleep that lasted well into the next day.

She finally completed her homeward journey, arriving in Whitby in mid-afternoon. The cottage was not in the town itself but a short drive along the coast toward Scarborough, nestling in a fold of the land with a view out over the farmland to Saltwick Nab. Originally a farm labourers residence, it stood alone at the end of a short track. Fiona stood for a moment taking in the distant murmur of the sea and the song of several birds, the fresh northeasterly wind in her face. Then she took out her keys and stepped through the door.

Diana, a neighbour who'd overseen the renting of the cottage, had ensured everything was spotless and, as agreed, had popped in the day before to stock the fridge. It took a few hours to get everything put away, then she settled herself in the big armchair by the main window with the view down to the Nab, it's familiar black outline gleaming wetly in the evening sunshine. She skimmed through the small pile of mail Diana had left by the front door. The sight of Imogen's handwriting brought a sudden pang of guilt. She'd promised to ring her as soon as she got back, and that was now three days ago. She glanced at her watch hoping it wasn't too late. The length of the summer evening had thrown her internal clock completely.

"Hello, Imogen, it's me, Fiona. Sorry I haven't rung before but I was tied up with meetings down in Birmingham. How are you? How's the exhibition opening gone?"

"Fiona! You are safely back, I was beginning to wonder. I'm fine and the exhibition is going really well. I've been hectic but it's really exciting. But how are you? Was it awful leaving Osubuso? What were you doing in Birmingham? And how does it feel to be home?"

The questions spilled out from them both, in Imogen's case simply because there was so much to catch up on, while Fiona's rush of words came more from nervousness at reestablishing this double- edged connection. The shared momentum kept them going for several minutes.

"So, when am I going to see you, then?" Imogen broached the underlying issue. "I'd come over right now, but I can't. I have to stay around the next few days to do my bit as a famous artist in the making." She laughed, "Not that I mind that, but I do mind that it stops me being with you. And I suppose you don't feel like upping sticks to come here when you've only just got back. So what shall we do?"

Eventually they agreed that Fiona would come across to Manchester the following Friday afternoon. "We could see a film, if you like, or go somewhere to eat. Have a lazy lie in on Saturday morning, or go round town, and you must come and see the exhibition before you go back. Whatever you fancy?" As ever Imogen was full of ideas and Fiona simply agreed with them all, not really having any idea what she might want to do among the myriad options presented.

35

Imogen waited impatiently on the platform. *"Of course the bloody train would be late, wouldn't it?"* She tried to be patient, walking to and fro like a caged tiger. At last the overhead speakers crackled out: 'The train now arriving at Platform 4 is the delayed 14.31 from York. We apologise ...' But Imogen's attention flitted from door to door as the passengers disembarked. There she was! She dashed down the platform to greet Fiona, thrusting a huge bunch of flowers into her hands, then crushing them in an enthusiastic embrace.

"Oh, it's so good to see you. Let me look at you properly," Imogen held her away for a moment, before pulling her close again. "You look tired. Have you had a terrible time with the trains? They're awful these days. Here, let me take your bag. I've got the car, it's out this way." She steered them towards the car park at the side of the station. "Just let me get the ticket. Oh, there's so much to tell you, I don't know where to begin. I've been hoarding all these thoughts in my head to share with you, and now there's nothing but jumble. I'm just so pleased to see you." She laughed at herself.

"Thanks for these, they're lovely. The journey wasn't too bad compared with STC in Ghana, besides I'm still not up to UK speed, so the delays just felt normal to me." Fiona smiled at Imogen, feeling both shy and excited. "It's good to see you too.

I'm looking forward to seeing your work tomorrow. What have you decided for tonight, in the end?"

As they drove out of town towards Chorlton, Fiona caught herself searching the crowds again, as she did in Whitby, reassured here by the comforting presence and familiarity of so many black faces. The readjustment to life in the UK was proving much more difficult and confusing than she'd anticipated. The pace of life constantly surprised her while the level of conspicuous consumption felt like a personal insult.

"Here we are. Welcome to the Palais Pollock." Imogen waved at a front door about three in from the end of a terraced row. "Come on in and we'll have a cup of tea. I told Carla to make herself scarce, so we should have the place to ourselves for a bit."

Imogen headed straight for the kitchen, pointing Fiona upstairs to the loo, "just put your bag in my room, it's the one at the front," she said, enjoying the thrill of anticipation the words created. While she waited for the kettle to boil she placed the flowers, now slightly the worse for wear, in a vase. She took out a packet of chocolate digestives and emptied them onto a plate, then added a Battenburg cake to the table. Both were favourites of Fiona's.

Fiona came back into the room as Imogen set out mugs and made the tea. "It's a lovely house, Imogen, and you've got so many beautiful photos everywhere. I could spend an age just looking at them, and all the other stuff, pottery, fabric, carvings. It's a real treasure trove."

"There we are, I let yours brew a bit longer, you like it stronger than me, I hope it's OK. We'll go out to eat later, but I thought you'd like a little something after the journey, so I got these. Help yourself." Imogen sat down, handing Fiona her tea. "How're you finding it being back home?"

Fiona swallowed a mouthful of cake before replying. "It's great in some ways. Everything's so easy, and available, and there's lots of little luxuries, like Battenburg cake," she smiled again, "but in other ways I'm finding it really weird. There's so much of everything, all at top speed and top volume. I've been finding it all a bit overwhelming, to be honest. Feeling like a fish out of water, which is silly, as I spent most of my life here."

"Yes, the rhythm of life in Osubuso is very different, isn't it?

You must miss them all terribly. I know I did when I came back last year, and you've been there so much longer." Imogen's sympathy was genuine, but she had not anticipated its effect on Fiona, who put her tea down as her eyes filled with tears. "I'm sorry," she managed, "but I miss it so much, Imogen, it's unbearable. I keep thinking this is unreal, and that I'll wake up back in Ghana, and everything will be fine again." She sniffed and took the box of tissues from Imogen's outstretched hand.

"Just give it time. You've only been back a week or so. Of course you're finding it difficult. But I'm really, really glad you're here, not in Osubuso." Imogen moved around the table to kneel next to Fiona's chair, taking the tissue from her to wipe her damp cheeks. "Aren't you just a little bit pleased to be here, I mean, there must be one or two things you were missing besides cake, surely?" she teased gently.

She was rewarded with a smile and a hug, which turned into something more passionate. "Yes, you're right, some things are better here." Fiona agreed several minutes later. "Tell me again what you've got planned for tonight."

"I thought we'd eat somewhere in the Village, then catch the late show at the Cornerhouse. There's a lesbian film on I'd like to see. You won't have heard of it, *Fire*, but it's really had excellent reviews. It's set and made in India. We'd need to be going in about half an hour. Is that OK?"

Fiona nodded.

It was a warm summer's evening and the Village was relatively quiet at this early hour. People called out to each other as they passed on the way from bar to bar. Imogen loved the free and easy atmosphere that existed in these few streets and tonight she felt a special pleasure dawdling along with Fiona at her side. Maybe they'd come back for a drink after the film, she thought hopefully, the place would be buzzing by then.

They ate in one of the quieter, more upmarket restaurants. Imogen, in the mood for celebration, was surprised when Fiona chose one of the plainest items on the menu. She raised a questioning eyebrow. "I know, I know, but I've been getting indigestion every time I have anything too rich. My stomach can't handle it." Fiona explained apologetically.

After the meal, they wandered along the canal-side. Imogen

spotted a group of friends and introduced Fiona. After an initial flurry of interest in her, their conversation moved easily onto the latest twists and turns in the relationships among their mutual friends, a controversial TV documentary, current celebrity gossip. Imogen was caught up in the chat, and quite failed to notice how little Fiona took part. Her attention was only caught when Fiona asked when it was the film started. With a promise to catch her friends up later, Imogen led the way the short distance to the cinema, chatting happily the whole time.

The film lived up to her expectations, leaving them both emotionally stirred in different ways. Imogen interpreted the film's ending in a positive light, sure that the two women had escaped to a new life together, while Fiona, more realistically she insisted, held to the view that one had perished. Knowing some of the friends they'd met earlier had also seen the film, Imogen was eager to find them and have a wider discussion. She persuaded Fiona to return to the Village.

However, when they found the group it was too noisy for any serious talk. In fact the pulsating music made any sort of conversation difficult. Fiona tried to enter into the spirit of the party, but she felt clumsy on the dance floor and the combination of noise, dim lighting and smoky atmosphere brought on a fierce headache. The constant gyration of bodies, the intensity of the focus on the music, and the distance she felt from the snatches of any conversation people did manage, left her feeling more alienated than if she'd been a Martian. She didn't want to spoil Imogen's evening, but after less than hour she was desperate. Catching Imogen's eye she mouthed a request to leave.

Luckily they had no trouble finding a cab. Imogen was contrite, "I should have remembered you get headaches, I'm so sorry. Why didn't you say something earlier, do you need some paracetamol?"

"No thanks, I just need to lie down. Sorry for being such a wimp."

In the bedroom, Imogen settled herself against the pillows. "Come here," she said quietly, "Lean back against me and I'll give you a head massage." Fiona let the gentle pressure of Imogen's fingers work their healing magic over her aching temples.

Moments later Fiona's breathing deepened and slowed.

Imogen was aware of the total relaxation of the warm body lying against hers. She moved carefully to a more comfortable position. Her disappointment at the way the evening of celebration had fizzled out was tempered by the steady rhythm of Fiona's breathing and the snug contact of an arm draped over her waist.

36

Fiona awoke just before six, the early start another Ghanaian habit. She slipped out of the bed and made her way down to the kitchen, careful not to wake either Imogen or Carla as she negotiated the unfamiliar route in the half light.

She sat at the table with a cup of tea trying to sort out the confusion in her head. It didn't seem to matter which part of her previous life she attempted to recapture: she felt a stranger to all of it. She felt more out of place and unsettled here in the land of her birth than she ever had in Ghana, even in those first few difficult weeks. She was appalled by so much of the world to which she'd returned. Extravagant, selfish, unthinking and hedonistic were the words that sprang immediately to mind. Reflecting on the night before she wondered anew about the wisdom of involvement with Imogen who had relished the atmosphere, the noise and commotion. She shook her head, puzzling over the vacuousness of Imogen's friends' chatter.

She admonished herself, '*Come on, they were having a night out on the town. It was neither the time nor the place for serious debate, and you know it. Don't judge them on such meagre and unfair evidence*'. But her irritation remained.

By about eight thirty Fiona had had enough of her own company. She filled the kettle again and took two mugs of tea back upstairs. At the sight of Imogen's semi-naked body sprawled across the bed a pulse of desire shot through her, providing her with one irresistible reason for pleasure at her return. Her conscious mind might fret over the whys and wherefores of the relationship, but no such doubts troubled her body. Forgetting all about the tea she had brought, she awoke

Imogen with sustenance of a different kind.

Quite some time later they made their way down to the kitchen. Carla was already there, toast in one hand, newspaper in the other. Several different papers lay scattered across the table. Imogen introduced the two of them. "Nice to meet you at last," Carla said through a mouthful of toast, "Imogen has said so much about you. I think of you as the Mother Theresa of Ghana." A wide teasing smile accompanied her words but Fiona expostulated even so. "Oh, that's ridiculous, there's no comparison."

"Well, no, I suppose not, after all, I wouldn't expect Mother Theresa to come down to breakfast with such a tell-tale rosy glow to her cheek." Carla laughed delightedly as a blush spread over Fiona's face. Imogen joined in the banter. "Just 'cos you're jealous now the tables are turned for once." She turned to Fiona, "Take no notice of Carla, she's not used to being the one without company on a Saturday morning. I've never known anyone with such a complicated love life. Even after, what, six, no eight months, I haven't quite worked out who is an ex, who is just a friend and who is the current soul-mate."

Carla laid a hand on her heart and assumed a stricken expression. "Oh, such hardness of heart, such indifference to my suffering. She knows the truth, Fiona, that I am forced to seek solace from others to heal the pain of her rejection." She glanced up from under her long lashes, flirting quite outrageously. "Now that I've met you, at last I understand why she has eyes for none but the fair Fiona." She took Fiona's hand and raised it to her lips with a flourish.

"Stop it, Carla." Imogen grinned at the dumbstruck expression on Fiona's face and reached an arm around her protectively, whispering in her ear. "Like I said, take no notice, she's quite insane, no hope at all of recovery." Fiona, unsure of how to join in what was so clearly an established pattern, picked up a section of the paper and let the banter pass unnoticed over her head.

An article on human trafficking caught her attention. "Bloody hell. Have you seen this, Imogen? There's some idiot writing in here that we should divert money from the aid budget to prevent illegal immigrants from swamping the country. Have you ever heard such a stupid idea?"

Carla said, "Oh, there's always someone banging on about illegal immigrants these days. It's just some politician's gimmick to pander to the whims of the great unwashed." She shook the tabloid paper she'd been reading. "This is where the interesting stuff is, gossip, dramatic true-life stories, and who's stabbing who in the back out there among the celebs. That's what keeps the world going round."

"But it does matter," Fiona rejected Carla's lighthearted response. "I mean, there's little enough money in the aid budget already. If this obsession with illegal immigrants goes on, then the money will move, and all that will do is increase the misery and lead to more migration. It's a thoroughly ignorant response to the problem."

"I know, honey, and so does whoever wrote that, probably. But polemic creates more impact than serious debate, makes more waves, gets a body noticed. So that's what they write." Carla shrugged and changed the subject. "Did you see the latest on the soap wars, Imo? Seems like they've got moles in every camp, leaking story lines all over the place. It says here that the big four soaps are heading for a showdown over who really has first dibs on the cloning plot. Both Channel 4 and Granada say their writers developed the story and then it was pinched by the others. Looks like it's going to get real nasty."

Imogen looked up from her own reading. "That's funny. In here they've got it the other way round. It's the Beeb that's claiming it was all their idea. They've even got a witness who supposedly overheard the mole at work. Look." She handed her version over to Carla and they examined the discrepancies in the stories together.

Fiona's good humour evaporated. How could Imogen devote so much energy to this and yet not even one word of response to the much more serious points she'd raised? "Christ Almighty! No wonder the real problems in the world just get worse and worse. Look at you, two intelligent adults with an obvious capacity for critical debate, and what do you spend your time worrying over? Bloody soap operas! Don't you ever look beyond the TV screen to think about the lives in the real world?"

"Blimey, who rattled your cage?" Carla said, amused by the ferocity of Fiona's attack.

Imogen took her words much more personally. "Shit a brick, Fiona. Don't you ever lighten up? It's not a crime to enjoy a soap opera, you know. It would probably do you the world of good. People need a bit of fun, something to balance all that doom and gloom you love. It does them good to go out, dance, get a bit drunk and just be bloody mindless now and again. The world's a nasty place, yes, but you don't have to ram that nastiness down our throats every other minute."

Fiona grew more angry. "No, of course not. God forbid that people should actually feel they had to do something about the nastiness. After all, it's so much easier to have fun, isn't it? And just forget about the rest of the world where the option doesn't even bloody well exist."

"Now just a minute. You know that's not fair. Not only because you're taking things out of context and out of proportion, but because you know full well that people everywhere take any opportunity they can to have fun, to find a bit of enjoyment in the dreariness of ordinary life. It's human nature."

Carla watched as the argument developed into a full scale row and insults of a more and more personal nature were thrown back and forth across the table. Used to a life of fiery emotional explosions, even she thought this a spectacular meltdown. It was no surprise when Fiona announced her intention to return to Whitby sooner than expected. The storm of words did not cease until the door slammed behind her.

Imogen stomped back into the kitchen. "Damn and fucking blast her. Why'd she have to go and spoil everything like that?" she said, sitting down and bursting into a flood of tears. Carla simply offered a silent shoulder.

Imogen stamped her way along the road trying to empty her mind. The success of the exhibition, pulling in a steady stream of appreciative customers hardly seemed important in the light of the weekend's events. She stopped trying to understand and gave in to anger. It seemed to be the only emotion of the many she was feeling that could find an outlet. She swung her foot at a tin can sending it bouncing crazily along the gutter. But what hurt most was that Fiona had left without visiting the Square Space Galleries. The exhibition only had one more week to run, making it likely that she would miss it altogether. She could forgive her a lot of things, Imogen reflected, but that would be nigh on impossible.

She took the steps to the Square Space doors two at a time, pausing at the top as she did every time to admire the poster which advertised her work: 'From Water To Dust, an exhibition of sculptures and photographs by Imogen Pollock, May 20 - June 7'. It wasn't quite having her name up in lights but it came a close second. The scowl left her face as she saw James coming toward her through the foyer.

James beckoned her over as she stepped through the door. "Imogen, are you ready for this? I just have to tell you. I can't keep it to myself a minute longer." He took her arm and pulled her through into his office, pushing her down into a chair. He stood before her smirking like a cat with a pint of double cream.

"Well, what is it?" Imogen said as the silence lengthened.

"Do you want the good news first or the brilliant?" James giggled as he sat on the edge of the desk enjoying her suspense. His foot twitched with barely suppressed excitement.

"I'd settle for average," Imogen said gloomily.

"Oh dear, not a good weekend, then?" James' expression was wry. He was aware of the importance she attached to Fiona's visit. "Never mind, pet. If you can't have happiness then maybe wealth will do."

"What do you mean?" Imogen's heart suddenly skipped a beat. Although there was nothing as vulgar as a price tag to be seen anywhere in the gallery, James kept a list in readiness against enquiries from prospective purchasers. "Has somebody...?"

"Somebody certainly has!" He clapped his hands together in glee. "A gentleman wishes to buy three pieces, all at the asking price. That means you'll get eleven hundred and fifty, after our commission."

Imogen was staggered. "Which ones does he want, who is he, when ..?" James held up his hands to stem the sudden flow of questions, then answered each one, ticking them off on his fingers as he did so. "He wants the two rickshaw pieces from the Bangladesh work and one set of the farming photos from Ghana. His name is Harold Endersby and he came in two days ago but has just confirmed his offer this morning on the phone."

"Wow." Imogen sat stunned, unable to take in the information, then she remembered. "Hang on, if that's just good news, then what on earth is the brilliant part?"

James beamed at her. "He owns a chain of restaurants called African Feast with an environmentally friendly, world citizen sort of theme, and he wants to commission you to provide sculptures for the decor in them. He has five already and is opening seven more in the next few months. He said something about going international, New York, Paris, or somewhere." James waved his hand in pretended indifference as if such places were as much part of his experience as Blackpool.

Imogen could only stare at him in amazement. "He said he would call later to get your answer and then you could arrange to meet and discuss the details further," James finished up. He took her hands and pulled her up from her seat to hug her tightly. "Congratulations, Imogen. Looks like you could be on your way."

Imogen floated out of James' office and wandered through the gallery unseeing. Her head was spinning with possibilities. Even Fiona was temporarily forgotten as she tried to absorb the implications of this sudden change in her fortunes. Mr Endersby rang the gallery as promised, speaking enthusiastically about Imogen's work and how he saw it fitting into his business. The restaurants reflected Mr Endersby's belief that while his customers deserved good food, this should not be at the expense of those who grew the ingredients, or the fertility of their land. A small proportion of his profits was devoted to encouraging ecological farming methods among the restaurants' mainly African suppliers. Imogen found him a persuasive man, determined to manage his business in line with his conscience. They agreed to meet to finalise a contract before the week was out.

When she got home Imogen found a scribbled note from Carla: F rang, v sorry, will ring again later. She sat down with the note in her hand, thinking about what it meant that Fiona had been the one to ring first. The calm woman with such surety of touch that Imogen had fallen in love with in Osubuso seemed to have disappeared, replaced by a confused and confusing mix of anger and depression. In the face of the change Imogen found it hard to be sure of her own feelings, although Saturday morning's lovemaking had been as good as anything they'd shared in Ghana. That thought brought a tingle to Imogen's spine: she wasn't ready to give up yet.

Impatient to restore harmony she picked up the phone and dialled Fiona's number. The initial apologies offered and accepted, Fiona broached the sensitive subject of her failure to visit the exhibition. "It was truly awful of me, just to storm out like that, and I know it means a lot to you. I really do want to see it. I could make it on Thursday afternoon." Fiona suggested.

"Damn, I've just arranged a meeting for Thursday. I haven't told you yet, but there's this guy who's bought a few of the pieces and he wants to commission some more. We're meeting to discuss the details on Thursday afternoon."

Fiona hid her disappointment. "But Imogen, that's wonderful. Congratulations. Maybe we could meet up a bit later?"

"Look, I'll come and join you at the Galleries as soon as I can. I don't think the meeting with Mr Endersby will be longer than a couple of hours at the most. If you get tired, just ask James to let you into the office and make you a cup of tea. He's always around somewhere."

"OK. See you Thursday then."

It was only after Fiona had rung off that Imogen remembered about the portrait. She'd been so sure that they'd be together when Fiona went round the exhibition that she'd stopped worrying about how she would react. She felt her anxiety return but given the uncertainty about any long term future between them, she decided to leave it to fate.

It was almost two when Fiona arrived at the Square Space Galleries. She was surprised by the size of the building, and her respect for Imogen's achievement grew as she took in the serious, professional atmosphere. "Can I help you?" A young woman appeared by her side.

"Yes, please. I'm interested in the exhibition by Imogen Pollock," said Fiona, feeling a peculiar sense of pride as she spoke the name.

"That's the exhibition on the first floor. The stairs are on the right. You can pick up information about all the exhibitions at the office, just down there." The woman pointed towards the rear of the building.

"Thank you." Fiona moved slowly up the stairs to the first floor. Several people were spread around the large square room. She stood for a moment, looking around without specifically focusing on any one object. This was all Imogen's work, this mix of sculpture and photography that people were studying with such fascination. A thrill ran through her as she began to work her way methodically round the collection.

The first few pieces came from Imogen's time in Dhaka and Fiona instantly saw the same skill at work as had been clear in the Osubuso book photography. The eye for detail and the ability to see through the surface to the hidden depths of people's lives. As with the book she was captivated by what she saw. Then, without warning, she was in front of a photo from Osubuso. The stab of recognition and homesickness was so acute she had to sit down. She was not going to lose control here, among strangers, but it took a huge effort of will to make herself continue. She blinked rapidly to clear her sight, then made her way into the second room following the clockwise direction indicated.

Two quite distinct sculptures were placed side by side on a white display plinth in the centre of the room. The label said 'out of water, back to dust: the circle of life'. The glaze on one sculpture glowed a deep greenish black, its surface incredibly smooth. The base was circular taking the form of a rippling pool and out of the middle rose the head and shoulders of a young girl with long straight hair, one strand trailing down over her cheek. The expression on the face was one of absolute delight. It was as if she was a naiad just breaking through from her underwater world. Fiona felt an almost overwhelming temptation to run her hands over the flowing surface, sure that they would come away wet.

The other half of the work was more abstract and at first Fiona could not make it out. The texture of the clay was rough and grainy. It was not glazed but had been fired to produce a rich glowing mix of ochreous reds and yellows along with more dirty looking metallic greys. From a forgotten portion of her brain the word 'raku' popped into Fiona's mind and she remembered Imogen saying something about a firing process which brought out these colours from oxides in the clay. As she looked at the sloping surface in front of her Fiona tasted the dust of the harmattan sharp on her tongue, and then as her eyes unfocused slightly she saw it. The cracks and crevices within the clay ground were not random. Just as the young girl rose from the water, here was an old woman embedded in the dusty earth, her face holding the wisdom of ages.

Fiona could not drag herself away for several minutes and when she did move on it was only to be caught by the sensuous curves of another piece. This was a rich, glowing chestnut colour, with variations of hue over the curves and bends of clay. Although the form was abstract Fiona was convinced it was some sort of human figure, but there seemed to be too many limbs. Puzzled she moved around it to see the title card. The name brought a lump to her throat and a renewed threat of tears pricked her eyes. The piece was labelled as 'chestnut babies'. Fiona heard Imogen's voice as clear as if she was in the room, the wonder in it as she looked down at the twins in the cot, two heads snuggling perfectly together.

'*I can't take much more of this*', she thought helplessly, but still she studied each remaining piece with infinite care. She moved toward the exit from the third room back to the first, thinking she had seen everything, when a couple came through a doorway in the far corner that she hadn't noticed. "But don't you think it's the best piece in the whole show?" one said vehemently as they walked passed her. Anxious not to miss anything Fiona went over to the corner and through the doorway.

Luckily, no one else came into the room, for they would have found Fiona, open-mouthed, staring transfixed at the portrait on the wall. How long she stood there, rooted to the floor, she had no idea, but the spell was only broken when a man entered from the opposite corner.

"It is Fiona, isn't it?" he inquired. "Imogen told me to look out for you. I'm sorry I didn't catch you when you came in, but I was busy in the office." Seeing Fiona's bewilderment he held out his hand. "I'm James, James Hughes."

Fiona closed her mouth and swallowed, automatically taking his proffered hand. She shook her head, unable to recover any sense of what she should do next. They were standing beside a portrait of her that was made up entirely of different shots of her naked body. And this man had been looking at it every day for the past three weeks at least. "Oh god." Fiona buried her face in her hands feeling the blush spread.

Realising something was amiss, James acted. Imogen had asked him to take care of Fiona, so that's what he should do. "Would a cup of tea help?" he asked gently. "My office is just down stairs, it's a bit more private for you than here." He took Fiona's arm.

"I'm sorry, you must think me very strange." Sitting in James' office with the familiar warmth of a cup of tea in her hands, Fiona said, "Imogen did tell me to look for you if I needed anything. Thank you for coming to my rescue like this."

"All part of the service," James offered with a smile. "But I think there was something she forgot to tell you about, wasn't there? Was it a shock?"

"You could say that, yes." Fiona warmed to him, liking his gentle manner, but only a small portion of her brain was engaged in the conversation.

Misinterpreting the cause of her reserve, and remembering Imogen's uncertainty about putting the portrait on display, James tried to protect his friend from any fall out. "I'm responsible for it being here, really. Imogen was very much in two minds. But it's such a powerful work. I knew that already, and meeting you confirms it. She's managed to catch something very particularly you in that portrait. You should be proud of it," he cleared his throat and continued, "although I realise you may feel a little sensitive about some of the smaller images. But the overall effect is perfect."

"Just at this moment, I don't know what I think or feel about any of it. It's knocked me completely off- balance. Not that I was feeling too steady before I came here, either." Fiona put down her cup and looked directly at James. "Imogen talks to you, doesn't she?" At his nod she went on, "then you'll know we're supposed to be meeting here later this afternoon."

James responded quickly, "Yes, she'll be here about four thirty, just over half an hour. I'm to keep you comfortable till then."

Fiona smiled wearily. "I'm sure in any other circumstances that would be my pleasure, but I can't stay. No, please," she raised a hand to forestall his protest. "I really do have to go, before I collapse completely. But you'll give Imogen a message for me, won't you?"

"Of course."

"Can you tell her that I think her work is wonderful, every single piece. That I'm utterly shattered by the impact it's had on me, but very proud of her." Fiona swallowed, barely holding on, but she knew she had to finish. "I'm sorry to run away again but if she can just be patient a little longer, I will sort myself out. Tell her that's a promise. And that I'd like her to come over to stay on Saturday. I won't run away a third time, that's another promise."

39

For the umpteenth time Imogen asked, "You're sure, absolutely sure that's what she said 'every single piece'?"

"Yes, I'm sure." Even James' patience was wearing thin. The last day of the exhibition had brought a rush of visitors and then they had stayed late to pack up. A new display was arriving in the morning so Imogen's work had to be removed that evening. It was an unusually speedy turn around for the gallery and it had been a long day. "And that she was proud of you, and she wanted you to go over and stay on Saturday, that's tomorrow. It really doesn't seem too bad to me."

"But why didn't she just stay here for another half an hour, then? If she wasn't upset by the portrait and if she liked my work so much, why couldn't she just have waited to tell me?" Imogen's voice betrayed both hurt and anger.

"I don't know, pet. All I know is what she told me to tell you, and that's what I've done. She said she was shattered and she looked it, but she wasn't angry or even upset really. Just exhausted. I can see why, if you question her as persistently as this whenever you see her."

"OK, OK, I get the message. I'm sorry. It just feels like my life is hanging in the balance a bit right now, that's all." Imogen looked round and counted the boxes. "I think everything's here. We might as well get it into the van and back home."

As they drove through the late summer evening to Chorlton, James asked about her meeting with Mr Harold Endersby. "You haven't really told me what he offered you, so come on, spill the beans."

"Well, it will be mainly photographic work, but he wants one sculpture for each restaurant, and I think he said he's got, or will have, twelve. He's already got the rickshaws, but they're for someone else so that means twelve more. The photos are to go on the walls, so we didn't agree a number. I still haven't really taken it in, and I've no idea how to go about actually doing it. I haven't really done much directly commissioned sculpture work."

"What about the money, honey? I want the detail." James grinned at her as he pulled the van to a halt outside her house. "Will it be enough to pay off the mortgage? Am I talking to a woman of substance now, and if so how do you feel about marriages of convenience?"

"I wish, no and not on your life in that order." Imogen jumped out of the van. "I'll tell you about the money if you get these inside while I put a bottle in the freezer. You can help me celebrate this, so that at least I've done it before anything else goes wrong."

Just a little while later she uncorked the wine and poured out two generous glasses. "Here's to me, to Square Space Galleries, and to you." She raised her glass in a salute, suddenly serious. "Especially to you, James, I couldn't have done it without your support. Thank you, for everything."

James lifted his glass in her direction and took a long swallow. "Mmm, very nice. Now quit the bullshit and tell me, how much?"

Imogen glowed with pleasure. "You're not going to believe it. The photos, however many they turn out to be, they're worth ten thousand, and the sculptures are three thousand each. That includes all the production and any travel costs, of course. And I've got to deliver it all by the end of next year."

James whistled. "Not bad at all, woman, not bad at all."

Imogen's delight bubbled over. "It isn't bad, is it, and depending on how the whole business takes off, he said there could be more in the future. But this is definite, at least once we've signed the contract and everything. So I'm going to be pretty busy over the next eighteen months, aren't I?"

"You are. Have you got any plans about where you'll go to get your inspiration? That sort of money should stretch quite a long way, I'd have thought."

Imogen sobered slightly. "No, I haven't got any idea. I'm not sure how to go about it, you see, both the other times I've gone away were through ActionFirst. I didn't have to think about any of the arrangements, or anything. It'll be a different matter trying to sort everything out myself."

"Oh, you'll be fine," James reassured her. "There's lots of good travel agents for that sort of thing now, and guide books, and there's always the internet if you get stuck for ideas or advice."

Carla came through from the sitting room to join in the party, pouring herself a generous glass of wine. She and James had established a pattern of flirtatious repartee that normally had Imogen in stitches, but after a while her mind returned to the implications of her work for Mr Endersby. If she was to meet the deadlines then she'd need to start thinking about where to go and what to look for sooner rather than later. She'd need to settle in a bit to each new place, get a feel for the pace of life before she'd be able to choose a successful subject, especially for the sculptures. It would mean several weeks away at a time. In the middle of this rather pleasing sequence of thought, another much less welcome notion intruded. Several weeks away meant several weeks apart from Fiona. She'd know after tomorrow whether that mattered or not, she supposed.

<u>40</u>

Fiona stared out of the window. The scudding grey clouds suited her mood. Her resolve to come to a decision before Imogen's visit the following day was strengthened by the arrival of a letter from Nigel in the morning's post. It contained a detailed description of the role they had discussed in outline in Birmingham.

Fiona put the letter in her pocket after giving it a quick skim through, and headed outside. She knew she needed a walk. It was the one thing she'd been unable to do in Ghana, where she had to invent other tactics when faced with difficult problems. None of those had brought her the same sense of ease. Walking produced a special combination of rhythmic movement and mental detachment that somehow unlocked even the most challenging of puzzles.

She made her way across the cliff from Saltwick Nab into Whitby noticing how much further the erosion had eaten into the farmland around the imposing ruins of the Abbey. She'd lost count of how many times the footpath had been re-routed to ensure walkers' safety. Coming down the steep Abbey steps, as always she found herself counting them, as if one day she'd find the number had changed.

Her route took her right through the centre of the small town. There were few people about at this early hour. Tomorrow, no doubt, the town would fill with day-trippers thronging in from Scarborough, Pickering and beyond. Tourism was the lifeblood of the economy here, Fiona knew, but she still liked it better in the off-season when the narrow streets weren't full of dawdling tourists, fretful children and unwary motorists.

She crossed the swing bridge and strode out towards the pier. She would not go home without walking right out to the end, but for now she took the slipway down onto the beach. The wide flat expanse stretched invitingly before her. The tide was about halfway out, Fiona thought, giving her time to get to Sandsend and back without danger of being cut off anywhere. She zipped her jacket back up to the neck. The strong northwesterly wind was much more noticeable down here away from the protection of the harbour and it was blowing right at her. She strode purposefully along eyes automatically scanning the pebble-strewn sand for anything that looked like a fossil. One windowsill back in the cottage held several specimens she'd picked up over the years.

A good hour and a half later she came back across the same stretch of sand under the watchful eye of the black cannons pointing out to sea. She climbed back up the ramp and turned out along the pier. Out at the end she turned her back to the sea and surveyed the scene in the other direction. The town nestled in between the two sides of the harbour in the shelter offered by the high cliffs. But it must have been a bleak life for the occupants of the Abbey so many centuries before, stuck out there on the headland exposed to every blast, she thought with a shudder. Despite her brisk pace she was cold. "Blood's got too thin out there in the tropical heat," she muttered to herself as she made her way back along the pier to the café for a cup of hot chocolate. She read Nigel's letter more thoroughly as she sipped her drink, paying attention to the details. Then she folded it back into her pocket and allowed this information to settle into her mind alongside everything else as she walked the remaining mile or two back to the cottage.

As she prepared her lunch she knew the walk had worked its usual miracle. She took her sandwich over to the armchair and examined the results of her morning's subconscious endeavour. First, and most definite, was the decision about Nigel's offer of long term work with ActionFirst. She wanted the job. She felt excited by the challenge of trying to adapt and adjust what she'd learned in Osubuso to other contexts. It would stretch her, demanding every ounce of her usual commitment and more, but the rewards would be huge. She knew her future lay in development work, and if she didn't get this job she would continue to look for something similar until she was successful.

That first decision made the second both more straightforward and more painful. '*Old habits die hard*'. Fiona reflected ironically as she saw yet again that she was allowing her work life to take precedence. True, the ActionFirst job would not be based overseas but it would involve several months of travel each year. She had no right to expect Imogen to find that an acceptable basis for a permanent relationship. So, if she was certain about spending her working life overseas for the foreseeable future then there was not much hope of that future including Imogen. And that's where the pain came in. Now she was faced with losing it, Fiona knew that a future with Imogen was something she did want. She wanted it very much.

'*So what now?*' She asked herself, and the third answer was just as clear as the previous two. Now she had to tell Imogen the two incompatible facts: that she loved her but that she was going to be spending half her life thousands of miles away from her. And she had to tell her in a way that didn't compromise Imogen's own decision, didn't push her into accepting less than she deserved or out of asking for what she wanted. '*It was honesty she asked you for in Ghana, and it's honesty she needs from you tomorrow. It will hurt and you'll feel embarrassed stating your feelings so clearly, but it's the least she deserves after the way you've treated her in the past few weeks. Time to bite the bullet, Fiona*'.

She spent the next little while working out a strategy for the visit.

41

Imogen pulled into the parking space and cut the engine. She almost gave in to an overwhelming surge of panic to switch back on and drive away but resisted, taking the key out of the ignition. She checked the note she'd made during Fiona's brief call that morning. The road to the cottage was easy to miss, she'd said, so why didn't they meet in Whitby itself. They could have lunch, maybe do a bit of shopping then Fiona could accompany her the last couple of miles. Imogen agreed, so they were due to meet at somewhere called the Crow's Nest in about ten minutes. Park near the Co-op supermarket, then go across the swing bridge and down the first street on the right, the instructions read. Imogen got out of the car, stretched and set off.

Just before she got to the bridge, the bells rang and the gate came down. She stood among the crowd of holiday makers and took the opportunity to study what she could see of the town.

Her eye followed the first tall-masted boat as it sailed through the open bridge past the sturdy fishing boats and out toward the open sea that sparkled beyond the harbour entrance. It was a very attractive prospect and her photographer's eye picked out one interesting angle after another. Turning her head to look inland she could just make out the tops of the moors in the distance.

Then the bridge reopened, she strode across and turned right. The butterflies in her stomach reached a crescendo as she saw Fiona standing at the door to the restaurant. Fiona's planning paid off, however, as the business of choosing from the menu gave them an obvious source of small talk, and the presence of other people kept them from becoming too intensely focused on each other. They even relaxed far enough to enjoy the food. After the meal they wandered through Whitby's streets in the warm afternoon sunshine. The sights and sounds gave them more than enough inspiration to keep their easy interaction going.

By the time another hour had passed, Fiona judged they were as ready as they ever would be to head home and deal with the serious business of the day. Inevitably the tension grew again as they drove the short distance to the cottage, but once there she created another brief breathing space by showing Imogen around. Then, finally the moment of truth arrived as they sat facing each other in the small sitting room. Fiona cleared her throat and embarked on the most difficult speech of her life.

"First of all I want you to know I was tremendously impressed with your work at the Galleries. I know you were very disappointed that I didn't stay to see you on Thursday, but I just had to be by myself. I knew from the Osubuso book that you had talent as a photographer, but your sculptures simply blew me away." She smiled at Imogen, "and then there was the portrait, of course. If James hadn't found me I'd probably still be standing there gawping."

"I hadn't told you about it because I thought I'd be the one to show it to you, then everything went pear-shaped. I was angry with you, and I didn't know whether it really mattered," Imogen explained, keeping her face impassive for once.

"I know, James did tell me you'd dithered about putting it on display, but he was right to encourage you. It's an ingenious piece of work. In a way I feel proud of it, almost like I made it myself, which is ridiculous, but you have every right to be proud of your work."

"Every artist needs inspiration. You provided mine." Imogen said quietly and her eyes held Fiona's for a moment as they both recalled the circumstances.

Recovering herself Fiona continued. "Anyway, your work crystallised something for me. That's why I had to leave. I had to digest it on my own. The power of your work and the passion you impart into every piece is really striking. It made me think about my own passion for work, and what it is I want to do. And my passion is for development work. Thanks to your exhibition I finally got that clear in my head."

"I could have told you that a year ago," Imogen said, this time with a slight smile. "It only took a few hours of watching you at work to see how well suited you were to it."

Fiona responded with a self-deprecating laugh. "I might even have known it a year ago too, but I'd lost sight of it since coming home, that's for sure. But it's the consequences of the realisation that I really need to make clear, what it means for us, or rather you." Seeing Imogen was about to speak again, she rushed on. "Please just let me get through this. If you stop me I might not have the courage to start again. I know I haven't ever seemed very sure that there was an 'us' and I wouldn't be surprised if you've doubted it too, just in the last week. But I've been doing some very serious thinking since Thursday. At the same time as I realised that I want a working life that will take me out of the country, I also realised that you are my love life." Fiona, remembering her vow not to influence Imogen's own decision, just managed to stop herself from saying 'the love of my life'. "Just before you left Ghana we had a conversation at the hotel, remember?" Imogen nodded and Fiona went on. "You said the most important thing was that we should be honest. So I have to tell you this isn't just a theoretical decision to be made in the future. Nigel has a job lined up with ActionFirst that he's pretty sure will be mine if I want it, and I do want it. That means I'd be out of the country for weeks at a time, and it would take a lot of my energy even when I was here. If there is to be an 'us' I want you to be clear that it would be on that sort of on-off basis, and if you want more, as you've every right to, then I want you to be honest about it too." At last Fiona felt she had said enough and she leant back in her chair with a deep sigh.

It was a moment or two before Imogen spoke, and Fiona watched in amazement as a smile spread more and more broadly across her face until she was positively beaming. "That's the second best news I've had this week, and if I tell you the first then you'll see why. I had that meeting with Mr Endersby on Thursday before we were due to meet, remember? God, it seems longer than two days ago. You're not the only one to be offered work. He's drawing up a contract for me to provide an unspecified number of photos and twelve sculptures for his new chain of restaurants called African Feast. And all of them have to link to that theme somehow, as well as with environment and development. The only thing that was worrying me was how I would make good enough contacts to find the subjects for the work, and you've just solved that for me."

Fiona smiled uncertainly. "How have I solved it?" she asked. "By getting another job with ActionFirst, you daft idiot, that means I can travel with you and capitalise on all your contacts. And probably if I do a few extra photos, Nigel will pay me too. He likes my work."

It took Fiona another few seconds to make all the connections that Imogen had made so quickly, then she said questioningly, "So ....?"

Imogen pulled Fiona to her feet, drawing her close. "There's an 'us' alright and nothing on-off about it. When you travel, I'll travel with you, when you're home, I'll work in the studio. Nothing's going to stop me from being your love life now." Imogen raised her hands to free the thick chestnut hair she loved so much. Fiona's agreement with her final statement was lost as their lips met.

Part Six: *Rich Harvest.*

42

Fiona stopped typing and reread the report she was working on. Then she clicked on 'save' and turned off the laptop. She stowed it safely in its bag. It was amazing what a transformation this one item had made to her life. She no longer wasted hours sitting at her old typewriter writing up the handwritten notes she'd made during a trip. Now she had the report virtually complete before she was even on the aeroplane. And the possibility of keeping in touch with the ActionFirst office by email meant that her trips to Birmingham had been cut by fifty percent. And all of that meant more time with Imogen.

She turned her head to where her partner was sitting on the other side of the hotel bedroom, updating her meticulous lists of the photos she'd taken. Despite Fiona waxing lyrical about the advantages of technology Imogen continued to use small leather bound notebooks to keep her records. "It's not that I'm a technophobe, you know how much stuff I've got in the darkroom, but these fit into my pocket and I can keep up to date without needing any power supply. If I don't write things down pretty soon after I take the shots, then I get muddled."

This was one of their longest trips since she'd taken up the job with ActionFirst almost a year before. The expansion of their work programme was spreading slowly through the African countries south of the Sahara. This trip had started in Malawi, then moved on to Zambia and they had spent the last three and a half weeks in Tanzania. It had been hard work as all three countries were new territory. Fiona often thought of how much she'd subconsciously learned about people management from Kofi Paul.

Imogen's work had been equally demanding. Each time they returned to the UK she would shut herself away for the first week or so, working in the darkroom, and transforming her sketches and ideas into three dimensional form. They had learned that separation was vital at such times, and, providing things went well on their return this time, Imogen would have the extra satisfaction of completing delivery three months ahead of schedule.

Fiona's gaze softened as she remembered the opening of the African Feast restaurant in Chester that they had attended just before leaving on this trip.

Although it offered the more common international stand-bys of Chinese, Indian or Mediterranean food, the key feature of Harold Endersby's restaurant chain, as the name indicated, was the range of African dishes, with choices from such cuisines as those of Ethiopia, Madagascar, Namibia or Mali.

Imogen's photographic work was displayed throughout the restaurant, and a sculpture took pride of place in the entrance. For the Chester outlet she'd created a small tableau of men and beasts threshing grain.

They had mingled among the guests and Imogen's nerves had finally settled as one after another made positive comments on her work. Fiona was filled with extraordinary pride as she basked in the reflected glory. But that was nothing to what she felt when Harold sprang the evening's big surprise.

"If I could just have your attention for a few moments, ladies and gentlemen," he tapped lightly on the side of a wine glass, and the hubbub subsided temporarily. "I'm sure all of you have already been impressed by the quality of the art work we have on display and I would like to formally introduce you to the very special woman who created it." He indicated Imogen who was seated beside him. "This is Imogen Pollock, and beside her, her partner Fiona Tisdale, another woman with exceptional gifts. I know from talking with Imogen that she feels it is only through her partnership with Fiona that she has come to fully understand the development processes that her work attempts to capture." Fiona blushed scarlet at this unexpected public accolade.

Harold went on. "So I am taking this opportunity to publicly thank Imogen for her work, not only for this restaurant but for the whole chain. Her creativity provides a very direct connection to the philosophy that underpins African Feast as a business, and which I know many of you support." There was a round of applause. He turned to Imogen again. "And now we have a surprise for you, someone else who wishes to express their appreciation of your work in a public way. One of our distinguished guests, Mr Toby Chambers."

Another round of applause greeted the new speaker as he took the microphone. Toby Chambers was a local TV personality best known for his sponsorship of the arts. Imogen turned to Fiona, whispering, "What does Harold mean? What's this about? Did you know anything about it?" but Fiona shook her head, "I don't know, honestly. Harold never mentioned anything."

Toby Chambers made some complimentary remarks about always being willing to accept free food and enjoying the general ambience of the event, then moved on. "But I'm actually here on official business. As you know I chair the panel of one of our most prestigious arts organisations here in the northwest, Arts in Focus, and it is in that capacity that I am delighted to stand before you this evening. I have admired Ms Pollock's work since her first exhibition at Square Space Galleries last year, and I believe her to be one of this regions truly outstanding creative talents." There was a murmur of agreement around the room. Imogen gripped Fiona's hand more tightly as she tried to retain her composure.

"Imogen, please, come and join me." Toby Chambers waved her up from her seat taking an envelope from his jacket pocket. "Ladies and gentlemen, it is my very real pleasure to announce that Imogen Pollock is the latest, highly deserving recipient of the Arts in Focus Outstanding New Artist Award." He handed Imogen the envelope as the audience erupted into loud applause and cheers. It contained a cheque for five thousand pounds.

It had taken days for Imogen to accept that the evening's events had been real. And now Fiona had another surprise of her own.

As Imogen put away her notebooks, Fiona went over and stood behind her, arms around her waist, lips nuzzling into her neck. "That's it, I'm done. Now we can get on with packing." Imogen said, turning within the circle of Fiona's arms. "Even though it's nice to be going home, I always feel sad at the end of a trip because it means I won't see you for days." Her hands cradled Fiona's face, "I seem to miss you more and more each time."

Fiona smiled into her lover's eyes. "Well, don't start missing me, not yet anyway, because we're not going home, not for a little while longer."

"Oh, why? Was there something in Nigel's email? What has he asked you to do now? I'll have to have another word with him about overloading you, he's always asking for just a little extra." Imogen stepped back searching her face for clues.

"Now don't you get started on Nigel again. For once he's quite innocent. I've arranged this all by myself. I've booked us on a flight in two week's time instead."

"You've what? But what about your meeting, isn't that next week?"

Fiona replied, "I've told Nigel I won't be there. I've sent him my comments by email."

Imogen raised her eyebrows. "Are you sure? I mean, you said it was going to be a key meeting this year because of the partnership issues. You're really going to miss it?"

Fiona laughed, "I know, you never thought you'd see the day, did you?" Imogen shook her head. "But, love of my life, it's true. We're going on safari instead, including a balloon ride over the Serengeti."

Imogen's excitement bubbled over in a stream of urgent questions but her crushing embrace prevented Fiona from finding the breath to answer.

* * * * *

Send for a free Onlywomen Press catalogue by writing to:
Onlywomen Press
Mail Order Department
40 St. Lawrence Terrace
London W10 5ST
England